Black Classics

D0839898

Laughing To Stop Myself Crying

Alice Dunbar Nelson

Published by *Black Classics*
An imprint of The X Press
6 Hoxton Square, London N1 6NU
Tel: 020 7729 1199
Fax: 020 7729 1771

Printed by Omnia Books Ltd, Glasgow, UK

Distributed in US by INBOOK, 1436 West Randolph Street, Chicago, Illinois 60607, USA Orders 1-800 626 4330 Fax orders 1-800 334 3892

Distributed in UK by Turnaround Distribution, Unit 3, Olympia Trading Estate, Coburg Road, London N22 6TZ
Tel: 020 8829 3000
Fax: 020 8881 5088

ISBN 1-874509-99-9

INTRODUCTION

Born Alice Ruth Moore on July 19, 1875 in New Orleans, the city that provides the local colour and backdrop for her characteristic fictional portraits of Creole life, Dunbar-Nelson was of mixed ancestry — black, white, creole and Native American — a gumbo of cultures which would subsequently inform her writing and lead her to create a multi-racial black short story tradition apart from the black and white minstrel stereotypes of the day.

She had reddish-blonde baby curls and a fair enough complexion to be able to 'pass' for white occasionally when, as an adult, she wished to partake in the high culture of museums, art galleries and operas from which America's 'Jim Crow' laws excluded her.

She was, nevertheless, a tireless campaigner for civil rights, as well as being the founder of the Industrial School for Colored Girls, which she launched with her own money.

After graduating from Straight College in 1892 Dunbar-Nelson went on to read at Cornell University, Columbia University and the University of Pennsylvania. She married and took the name of the celebrated poet Paul Laurence Dunbar in 1898, a marriage that lasted just four years. Her first book *Violets and Other Tales* included essays, poems and short stories. The second *The Goodness of St. Roque* (1898) was the first collection of short stories to be published by an African-American woman. She later became the first African-American woman to be elected to the Delaware Republican State Committee.

Dunbar-Nelson was writing at a time when things were extremely difficult for black women writers in the face of a hostile literary establishment. To support herself she worked variously as a teacher, journalist, secretary, stenographer, and campaign manager. She died in 1935.

Laughing To Stop Myself Crying, is a compilation of the best from *Violets and Other Tales* and *The Goodness of St. Roque*.

Yvette Richards, June 2000, London.

SISTER JOSEPHA

SISTER JOSEPHA held her beads mechanically, her fingers numb with the accustomed exercise. The little organ creaked a dismal "O Salutaris," and she still knelt on the floor, her white-bonneted head nodding suspiciously. The Mother Superior gave a sharp glance at the tired figure. Then, as a sudden lurch forward brought the little sister back to consciousness, Mother's eyes relaxed into a genuine smile.

The bell tolled the end of vespers, and the sombre-robed nuns filed out of the chapel to go about their evening duties. Little Sister Josepha's work was to attend to the household lamps, but there must have been as much oil spilled upon the table tonight as was put in the vessels. The small brown hands trembled so that most of the wicks were trimmed with points at one corner which caused them to

1

smoke that night.

"Oh, *cher Seigneur*," she sighed, giving an impatient polish to a refractory chimney, "it is wicked and sinful, I know, but I am so tired. I can't be happy and sing any more. It doesn't seem right for *le bon Dieu* to have me all cooped up here with nothing to see but stray visitors, and always the same old work, teaching those mean little girls to sew, and washing and filling the same old lamps. Pah!"

They were rebellious prayers that the red mouth murmured that night, and a restless figure that tossed on the hard dormitory bed. Sister Dominica called from her couch to know if Sister Josepha were ill.

"No," was the somewhat short response. Then a muttered, "Why can't they let me alone for a minute? That pale-eyed Sister Dominica never sleeps. That's why she is so ugly."

About fifteen years before this night someone had brought to the orphan asylum connected with this convent, du Sacre Coeur, a round, dimpled bit of three-year-old humanity, who regarded the world from a pair of gravely twinkling black eyes, and only took a chubby thumb out of a rosy mouth long enough to answer in monosyllabic French. It was a child without an identity. There was but one name that anyone seemed to know, and that, too, was vague — Camille.

She grew up with the rest of the waifs; scraps of French and American civilization thrown together to develop a seemingly inconsistent miniature world. Mademoiselle Camille was queen among them, a pretty little tyrant who ruled the children and dominated the more timid sisters in charge.

One day an awakening came. When she was fifteen, and almost fully ripened into a glorious tropical beauty of the type that matures early, some visitors to the convent were fascinated by her and asked the Mother Superior to give the girl into their keeping.

Camille fled like a frightened fawn into the yard, and was only unearthed with some difficulty from behind a group of palms. Sulky and pouting, she was led into the parlour, picking at her blue pinafore like a spoiled infant.

"The lady and gentleman wish you to go home with them, Camille," said the Mother Superior, in the language of the convent. Her voice was kind and gentle apparently. But the child, accustomed to its various inflections, detected a steely ring behind its softness, like the proverbial iron hand in the velvet glove.

"You must understand, madame," continued Mother, in stilted English, "that we never force children from us. We are ever glad to place them in comfortable — how you say that — quarters, *maisons*, homes. *Bien!* But we will not make them go if they do not wish."

Camille stole a glance at her would-be guardians, and decided instantly, impulsively, finally. The woman suited her; but the man! It was doubtless intuition of the quick, vivacious sort which belonged to her blood that served her. Untutored in worldly knowledge, she could not divine the meaning of the pronounced leers and admiration of her physical charms which gleamed in the man's face, but she knew it made her feel creepy, and stoutly refused to go.

Next day Camille was summoned from a task to the Mother Superior's parlour. The other girls gazed with envy upon her as she dashed down the courtyard with impetuous movement. Camille, they decided crossly, received too much notice. It was Camille this, Camille that; she was pretty, it was to be expected. Even Father Ray lingered longer in his blessing when his hands pressed her silky black hair.

As she entered the parlour, a strange chill swept over the girl. The room was not an unaccustomed one, for she had swept it many times, but today the stiff black chairs, the dismal crucifixes, the gleaming whiteness of the walls, even the cheap lithograph of the Madonna which Camille had always regarded as a perfect specimen of art, seemed cold and mean.

"Camille, *ma chere*," said Mother, "I am extremely displeased with you. Why did you not wish to go with Monsieur and Madame Lafaye yesterday?"

The girl uncrossed her hands from her bosom, and spread them out in a deprecating gesture.

"*Mais, ma mère*, I was afraid."

Mother's face grew stern. "No foolishness now," she exclaimed.

"It is not foolishness, *ma mère*. I could not help it, but that man looked at me so funny, I felt all cold chills down my back. Oh, dear Mother, I love the convent and the sisters so, I just want to stay and be a sister too, may I?"

And thus it was that Camille took the white veil at sixteen years. Now that the period of novitiate was over, it was just beginning to dawn upon her that she had made a mistake.

"Maybe it would have been better had I gone with

the funny-looking lady and gentleman," she mused bitterly one night. "Oh, Seigneur, I'm so tired and impatient. It's so dull here and, dear God, I'm so young."

There was no help for it. One must arise in the morning and help in the refectory with the stupid Sister Francesca, and go about one's duties with a prayerful mien, and not even let a sigh escape when one's head ached with the eternal telling of beads.

A great fête day was coming, and an atmosphere of preparation and mild excitement pervaded the brown walls of the convent like a delicate aroma. The old Cathedral around the corner had stood a hundred years, and all the city was rising to do honour to its age and time-softened beauty. There would be a service with two Cardinals, and Archbishops and Bishops, and all the accompanying glitter of soldiers and orchestras. The little sisters of the Convent du Sacre Coeur clasped their hands in anticipation of the holy joy. Sister Josepha curled her lip, she was so tired of churchly pleasures.

The day came, a gold and blue spring day, when the air hung heavy with the scent of roses and magnolias, and the sunbeams fairly laughed as they kissed the houses. The old Cathedral stood gray and solemn, and the flowers in Jackson Square smiled cheery birthday greetings across the way. The crowd around the door surged and pressed and pushed in its eagerness to get within. Ribbons stretched across the banquette were of no avail to repress it, and important ushers with cardinal colours could do little more.

The Sacred Heart sisters filed slowly in at the side door, creating a momentary flutter as they paced reverently to their seats, guarding the blue-bonneted orphans. Sister Josepha, determined to see as much of the world as she could, kept her big black eyes opened wide, as the church rapidly filled with the fashionably dressed, perfumed, rustling, and self-conscious throng.

Her heart beat quickly. The rebellious thoughts that will arise in the most philosophical of us surged in her small heavily gowned bosom. For her were the gray things, the neutral tinted skies, the ugly garb, the coarse meats. For them the rainbow, the ethereal airiness of earthly joys, the bonbons and glaces of the world. Sister Josepha did not know that the rainbow is elusive, and its colours but the illumination of tears. She had never been told that earthly reality is necessarily ephemeral, nor that bonbons and glaces, whether of the palate or of the soul, nauseate and pall upon the taste. Dear God, forgive her, for she bent with contrite tears over her worn rosary, and glanced no more at the worldly glitter of femininity.

The sunbeams streamed through the high windows in purple and crimson lights upon a veritable fugue of colour. Within the seats, crush upon crush of spring millinery; within the aisles erect lines of gold-braided, gold-buttoned military. Upon the altar, broad sweeps of golden robes, great dashes of crimson skirts, mitres and gleaming crosses, the soft neutral hue of rich lace vestments, the tender heads of childhood in picturesque attire. The proud, golden magnificence of the domed altar with its weighting mass of lilies and wide-eyed roses, and the long candles that sparkled their yellow star points above the reverent throng within the altar rails.

The soft baritone of the Cardinal intoned a single phrase in the suspended silence. The censer took up the note in its delicate clink clink, as it swung to and fro in the hands of a fair-haired child. Then the organ, pausing an instant in a deep, mellow, long-drawn note, burst suddenly into a magnificent strain, and the choir sang forth, "Kyrie Eleison, Christe Eleison." One voice, flute-like, piercing, sweet, rang high over the rest. Sister Josepha heard and trembled, as she buried her face in her hands, and let her tears fall, like other beads, through her rosary.

It was when the final word of the service had been intoned, the last peal of the exit march had died away, that she looked up meekly, to encounter a pair of youthful brown eyes gazing pityingly upon her. That was all she remembered for a moment, that the eyes were youthful and handsome and tender. Later, she saw that they were placed in a rather beautiful boyish face surmounted by waves of brown hair, curling and soft, and that the head was set on a pair of shoulders decked in military uniform. Then the brown eyes marched away with the rest of the rear guard, and the white-bonneted sisters filed out the side door, through the narrow court, back into the brown convent.

That night Sister Josepha tossed more than usual on her hard bed, and clasped her fingers often in prayer to quell the wickedness in her heart. Turn where she would, pray as she might, there was ever a pair of tender, pitying brown eyes, haunting her persistently. The squeaky organ at vespers intoned the clank of military accoutrements to her ears, the white bonnets of the sisters about her faded into mists of curling brown hair. Briefly, Sister Josepha was in love.

The days went on pretty much as before, save for the one little heart that beat rebelliously now and then, though it tried so hard to be submissive. There was the morning work in the refectory, the stupid little girls to teach sewing, and the insatiable lamps that were so greedy for oil. And always the tender, boyish brown eyes, that looked so sorrowfully at the fragile, beautiful little sister, haunting, following, pleading.

Perchance, had Sister Josepha been in the world, the eyes would have been an incident. But in this home of self-repression and retrospection, it was a life story. The eyes had gone their way, doubtless forgetting the little sister they pitied, but the little sister? The days glided into weeks, the weeks into months. Thoughts of escape had come to Sister Josepha, to flee into the world, to merge in the great city where recognition was impossible, and, working her way like the rest of humanity, perchance encounter the eyes again.

It was all planned and ready. She would wait until some morning when the little band of black-robed sisters wended their way to mass at the Cathedral.

When it was time to file out the side door into the courtway, she would linger at prayers, then slip out another door, and unseen glide up Chartres Street to Canal, and once there, mingle in the throng that filled the wide thoroughfare. Beyond this first plan she could think no further. Penniless, garbed, and shaven though she would be, other difficulties never presented themselves to her. She would rely on the mercies of the world to help her escape from this torturing life of inertia. It seemed easy now that the first step of decision had been taken.

The Saturday night before the final day had come, and she lay feverishly nervous in her narrow little bed, wondering with wide-eyed fear at the morrow. Pale-eyed Sister Dominica and Sister Francesca were whispering together in the dark silence, and Sister Josepha's ears pricked up as she heard her name.

"She is not well, poor child," said Francesca. "I fear the life is too confining."

"It is best for her," was the reply. "You know, sister, how hard it would be for her in the world, with no name but Camille, no friends, and her beauty; and then—"

Sister Josepha heard no more, for her heart beating tumultously in her bosom drowned the rest. Like the

rush of the bitter salt tide over a drowning man
clinging to a spar, came the complete submerging of
her hopes of another life. No name but Camille, that
was true; no nationality, for she could never tell from
whom or whence she came. No friends, and a beauty
that not even an ungainly bonnet and shaven head
could hide. In a flash she realised the deception of the
life she would lead, and the cruel self-torture of
wonder at her own identity. Already, as if in
anticipation of the world's questionings, she was
asking herself, "Who am I? What am I?"

The next morning the sisters du Sacre Coeur filed
into the Cathedral at High Mass, and bent devout
knees at the general confession. *"Confiteor Deo
omnipotenti,"* murmured the priest, and tremblingly
one little sister followed the words, *"Je confesse a Dieu,
tout puissant, que j'ai beaucoup peche par pensées, c'est
ma faute, c'est ma faute, c'est ma très grande faute."*

The organ pealed forth as mass ended, the throng
slowly filed out, and the sisters paced through the
courtway back into the brown convent walls. One
paused at the entrance, and gazed with swift longing
eyes in the direction of narrow, squalid Chartres
Street, then, with a gulping sob, followed the rest,
and vanished behind the heavy door.

THE PRALINE WOMAN

THE praline woman sits by the side of the Archbishop's quaint little old chapel on Royal Street, and slowly waves her latanier fan over the pink and brown wares.

"Pralines, pralines. Ah, ma'amzelle, you buy? *S'il vous plait*, ma'amzelle, ces pralines, they be fine, very fresh."

"*Mais non*, maman, you are not sure?

"Sho', chile, ma bebe, ma petite, she put these up hissef. His hand's so small, ma'amzelle, like yours, *mais brune*. She put these up this morning. You take none? No husband for you then!"

"Ah, *ma petite*, you take? *Cinq sous, bebe*, may *le bon Dieu* keep you good!"

"*Mais oui*, madame, I know you *etranger*. You don't look like these New Orleans people. You look like those Yankee that come down before the war."

Ding-dong, ding-dong, ding-dong, chimes the Cathedral bell across Jackson Square, and the praline woman crosses herself.

"Hail, Mary, full of grace."

"Pralines, madame? You buy like that? Dix sous, madame, and one little piece of lagniappe for madame's little bebe. Ah, *c'est bon!*

"Pralines, pralines, so fresh, so fine! M'sieu would like some for his lil' gal' at home? *Mais non*, what's that you say? She's dead! Ah, m'sieu, 't is my lil' gal what died long year ago. *Misere, misere!*

"Here come that lazy Indian squaw. What she good for, anyhow? She jes' sit like that in the French Market and sleep, sleep, sleep, like so in her blanket. Hey there, you, Tonita, how goes your business?

"Pralines, pralines! Holy Father, you give me that blessing sho'? Take one, I know you like that white one. It taste good, I know, bien.

"Pralines, madame? I like your face. What for you wear black? Your lil' boy dead? You take one, jes' see how it taste. I had one lil' boy once, he jes' grow until he's big like this, then one day he take sick and die. Oh, madame, it mos' broke my poor heart. I burn candle in St. Rocque, I say my beads, I sprinkle holy water round his bed. His eyes turn up, he say 'Maman,' then he die. Madame, you take one. *Non, non*, no *l'argent*, you take one for my lil' boy's sake.

"Pralines, m'sieu? Who make these? My lil' gal, Didele, of course. *Non, non,* I don't make no mo'.'"

Poor Tante Marie get too old. Didele? She's one lil' gal I adopt. I see her one day in the street. He walk so;

it cold she shiver, and I say, 'Where you gone, lil' gal?' and she can't tell. She jes' come close to me, and cry so. Then I take her home with me, and she say he's name Didele. You see, there weren't nobody there. My lil' gal, she's dead of yellow fever, my lil' boy, he's dead, poor Tante Marie all alone. Didele, she grow fine, she keep house and makes pralines. Then, when night come, she sit with her guitar and sing:

Tu l'aime ces trois jours
Tu l'aime ces trois jours
Ma cour a toi
Tu l'aime ces trois jours.

"Ah, he's fine gal, is Didele. Pralines, pralines! That lil' cloud, it look like rain, I hope no. Here come that lazy Irishman down the street. I don't like Irishman, me, *non*, they so funny. One day one Irishman, he say to me, 'Auntie, what for you talk so?' and I jes' say back, 'What for you say "Faith an' be jabers"?' *Non*, I don't like Irishman, me!

"Here come the rain. Now I got for to go. Didele, she be wait for me. Down it come. It fall in the Mississippi, and fill up clean to the levee. *Bonjour*, madame, you come again? Pralines! Pralines!"

MR. BAPTISTE

HE might have had another name, we never knew. Someone had christened him Mr. Baptiste long ago in the dim past, and it sufficed. No one had ever been known who had the temerity to ask him for another cognomen, for though he was a mild-mannered little man, he had an uncomfortable way of shutting up oyster-wise and looking disagreeable when approached concerning his personal history.

He was small: most Creole men are small when they are old. It is strange, but a fact. It must be that age withers them sooner and more effectually than those of un-Latinised extraction. Mr. Baptiste was, furthermore, very much wrinkled and lame. Like the Son of Man, he had nowhere to lay his head, save when some kindly family made room for him in a garret or a barn. He subsisted by doing odd jobs, whitewashing, cleaning yards, doing errands, and the like.

The little old man was a frequenter of the levee. Never a day passed that his quaint little figure was not seen moving up and down about the ships. Chiefly did he haunt the Texas and Pacific warehouses and the landing-place of the Morgan-line steamships. This seemed like madness, for these spots are almost the busiest on the levee, and the rough seamen and 'longshoremen have least time to be bothered with small weak folks. Still there was method in the madness of Mr. Baptiste. The Morgan steamships, as everyone knows, ply between New Orleans and Central and South American ports, doing the major part of the fruit trade, and many were the baskets of forgotten fruit that Mr. Baptiste took away with him unmolested. Sometimes, you know, bananas and mangoes and oranges and citrons will half spoil, particularly if it has been a bad voyage over the stormy Gulf, and the officers of the ships will give away stacks of fruit, too good to go into the river, too bad to sell to the fruit-dealers.

You could see Mr. Baptiste trudging up the street with his quaint one-sided walk, bearing his dilapidated basket on one shoulder, a nondescript headcover pulled over his eyes, whistling cheerily. Then he would slip in at the back door of one of his clients with a brisk, "Ah, *bonjour*, madame. Now here is jus' a little bit of fruit, some bananas. Perhaps madame would cook some for Mr. Baptiste?"

And madame, who understood and knew his ways, would fry him some of the bananas, and set it

before him, a tempting dish, with a bit of madame's
bread and meat and coffee thrown in. Mr. Baptiste
would depart, filled and contented, leaving the load
of fruit behind as madame's pay. Thus did he eat, and
his clients were many, and never too tired or too cross
to cook his meals and get their pay in baskets of fruit.

One day he slipped in at Madame Garcia's kitchen
door with such a woebegone air, and slid a small sack
of nearly ripe plantains on the table with such a
misery-laden sigh, that madame, who was fat and
excitable, threw up both hands and cried out:

"*Mon Dieu*, Mister Baptiste, why do you look like
that? What is the matter?"

For answer, Mr. Baptiste shook his head gloomily
and sighed again. Madame Garcia moved heavily
about the kitchen, putting the plantains in a cool spot
and punctuating her footsteps with sundry "*Mon
Dieux*" and "*Miseres.*"

"Dose cotton," ejaculated Mr. Baptiste, at last.

"Ah, *mon Dieu*," groaned Madame Garcia, rolling
her eyes heavenwards.

"It will drive the fruit away!" he continued.

"*Misere!*" said Madame Garcia.

"It will."

"*Oui, oui,*" said Madame Garcia. She had carefully

inspected the plantains, and seeing that they were good and wholesome, was inclined to agree with anything Mr. Baptiste said.

He grew excited.

"Yes, dose cotton yardmen, dose longshoremen, they go out on one strike. They throw down their tools and say they work no mo' with niggers. *Les veseaux*, they lay in the river, no work, no cargo, yes. Then the men, they threaten and say things. They make big fight, yes. There's no mo' work on the levee, like that. Everybody jus' walk round and say cuss word, yes!"

"Oh, *mon Dieu, mon Dieu*," groaned Madame Garcia, rocking her guineablue-clad self to and fro.

Mr. Baptiste picked up his nondescript head-cover and walked out through the brick-reddened alley, talking excitedly to himself. Madame Garcia called after him to know if he did not want his luncheon, but he shook his head and passed on.

Down on the levee it was even as Mr. Baptiste had said. The longshoremen, the cotton-yardmen, and the stevedores had gone out on a strike. The levee lay hot and unsheltered under the glare of a noonday sun. The turgid Mississippi scarce seemed to flow, but gave forth a brazen gleam from its yellow bosom.

Great vessels lay against the wharf, silent and unpopulated. Excited groups of men clustered here and there among bales of uncompressed cotton, lying about in disorderly profusion. Cargoes of molasses and sugar gave out a sticky sweet smell, and now and then the fierce rays of the sun would kindle tiny blazes in the cotton and splinter-mixed dust underfoot.

Mr. Baptiste wandered in and out among the groups of men, exchanging a friendly salutation here and there. He looked the picture of woe-begone misery.

"Hello, Mr. Baptiste," cried a big, brawny Irishman, "sure and you look, as if you was about to be hanged."

"Ah, mon Dieu," said Mr. Baptiste, "dose fruit ship be ruined for this strike."

"Damn the fruit," cheerily replied the Irishman, artistically disposing of a mouthful of tobacco juice. "It ain't the fruit we care about, it 's the cotton."

"Hear! Hear!" cried a dozen lusty comrades.

Mr. Baptiste shook his head and moved sorrowfully away.

"Hey, by holy St. Patrick, here's that little fruit-eater," called the centre of another group of strikers perched on cotton-bales.

"Hello! Where—" began a second. But the leader suddenly held up his hand for silence, and the men listened eagerly.

It might not have been a sound, for the levee lay quiet and the mules on the cotton-drays dozed languidly, their ears pitched at varying acute angles. But the practised ears of the men heard a familiar sound stealing up over the heated stillness.

"Oh humph!"

Then the faint rattle of chains, and the steady thump of a machine pounding.

If ever you go on the levee you'll know that sound, the rhythmic song of the stevedores heaving cotton-bales, and the steady thump,thump, of the machine compressing them within the hold of the ship.

Finnegan, the leader, who had held up his hand for silence, uttered an oath.

"Scabs! Men, come on."

There was no need for a further invitation. The men rose in sullen wrath and went down the levee, the crowd gathering in numbers as it passed along. Mr. Baptiste followed in its wake, now and then sighing a mournful protest which was lost in the roar of the men.

"Scabs!" Finnegan had said. The word was passed along, until it seemed that the half of the second District knew and had risen to investigate.

"Oh humph!"

The rhythmic chorus sounded nearer, and the cause manifested itself when the curve of the levee above the French Market was passed. There rose a White Star steamer, insolently settling itself to the water as each consignment of cotton bales was compressed into her hold.

"Niggers!" roared Finnegan angrily.

"Niggers! Kill 'em, scabs!" chorused the crowd.

With muscles standing out like cables through their blue cotton shirts, and sweat rolling from glossy black skins, the Negro stevedores were at work steadily labouring at the cotton, with the rhythmic song swinging its cadence in the hot air. The roar of the crowd caused the men to look up with momentary apprehension, but at the overseer's reassuring word they bent back to work.

Finnegan was a Titan. With livid face and bursting veins he ran into the street and uprooted a huge block of paving stone. Staggering under its weight, he rushed back to the ship, and with one mighty effort hurled it into the hold.

The delicate poles of the costly machine tottered in the air, then fell forward with a crash as the whole iron framework in the hold collapsed.

"Damn ye," shouted Finnegan, "now yez can pack yer cotton!"

The crowd's cheers at this changed to howls, as the Negroes, infuriated at their loss, for those costly machines belong to the labourers and not to the ship owners, turned upon the mob and began to throw brickbats, pieces of iron, chunks of wood, anything that came to hand. It was pandemonium turned loose over a turgid stream, with a malarial sun to heat the passions to fever point.

Mr. Baptiste had taken refuge behind a bread-stall on the outside of the market. He had taken off his cap, and was weakly cheering the Negroes on.

"Bravo," cheered Mr. Baptiste.

"Will yez look at that damned fruit-eating Frenchman!" howled McMahon. "Cheering the niggers, are you?" and he let fly a brickbat in the direction of the bread stall.

"*Mon Dieu, mon Dieu,*" wailed the bread woman.

Mr. Baptiste lay very still, with a great ugly gash in his wrinkled brown temple. Fishmen and vegetable merchants gathered around him in a quick, sympathetic mass. The individual, the concrete bit of helpless humanity, had more interest for them than the vast, vague fighting mob beyond.

The noon-hour pealed from the brazen throats of many bells, and the numerous hoarse whistles of the steamboats called the unheeded luncheon time to the levee workers. The war waged furiously, and groans of the wounded mingled with curses and roars from the combatants.

"Killed instantly," said the surgeon, carefully lifting Mr. Baptiste into the ambulance.

Tramp, tramp, tramp, sounded the militia steadily marching down Decatur Street.

"Wait, do yez hear!" shouted Finnegan, and the conflict had ceased before the yellow river could reflect the sun from the polished bayonets.

You remember, of course, how long the strike lasted, and how many battles were fought and lives lost before the final adjustment of affairs. It was a fearsome war, and many forgot afterwards whose was the first life lost in the struggle — poor little Mr. Baptiste's, whose body lay at the morgue unclaimed for days before it was finally dropped unnamed into Potter's Field.

TONY'S WIFE

"GIMME fi' cents worth of candy, please."

It was the little Jew girl who spoke, and Tony's wife roused herself from her knitting to rise and count out the multi-hued candy which should go in exchange for the dingy nickel grasped in warm, damp fingers. Three long sticks, carefully wrapped in crispest brown paper, and a half dozen or more of pink candy fish, and the little Jew girl sped away in blissful contentment. Tony's wife resumed her knitting with a stifled sigh until the next customer should come.

A low growl caused her to look up apprehensively. Tony himself stood beetle-browed and huge in the small doorway.

"Get up from there," he muttered, "and open two dozen oysters right away, the Eliots want 'em."

His English was unaccented. It was long since he had seen Italy.

She moved meekly behind the counter, and began work on the thick shells. Tony stretched his long neck up the street.

"Mr. Tony, mama wants some charcoal." The very small voice at his feet must have pleased him, for his black brows relaxed into a smile, and he poked the little one's chin with a hard, dirty finger, as he emptied the ridiculously small bucket of charcoal into the child's bucket, and gave a banana for lagniappe.

The crackling of shells went on behind, and a stifled sob arose as a bit of sharp edge cut into the thin, worn fingers that clasped the knife.

"Hurry up there, will you?" growled the black brows. "The Eliots are sending for the oysters."

She deftly strained and counted them, and, after wiping her fingers, resumed her seat, and took up the endless crochet work, with her usual stifled sigh.

Tony and his wife had always been in this same little queer old shop on Prytania Street, at least to the memory of the oldest inhabitant in the neighbourhood. When or how they came, or how they stayed, no one knew. It was enough that they were there, like a sort of ancestral fixture to the street. The neighbourhood was fine enough to look down upon these two tumble-down shops at the corner, kept by Tony and Mrs. Murphy, the grocer. It was a semi-fashionable locality, far up-town, away from the old-time French quarter. It was the sort of neighbourhood where millionaires live before their fortunes are made and fashionable, high-priced private schools flourish, where the small cottages are occupied by aspiring schoolteachers and choir-singers. Such was this locality, and you must admit that it was indeed a condescension to tolerate Tony and Mrs. Murphy.

He was a great, black-bearded, hoarse-voiced, six-foot specimen of Italian humanity, who looked in his little shop and on the prosaic pavement of Prytania Street somewhat as Hercules might seem in a modern drawing-room. You instinctively thought of wild mountain-passes, and the gleaming dirks of bandit contadini in looking at him. What his last name was, no one knew. Someone had maintained once that he had been christened Antonio Malatesta, but that was unauthentic, and as little to be believed as that other wild theory that her name was Mary.

She was meek, pale, little, ugly, and German. Altogether part of his arms and legs would have very decently made another larger than she. Her hair was pale and drawn in sleek, thin tightness away from a pinched, pitiful face, whose dull cold eyes hurt you, because you knew they were trying to mirror sorrow, and could not because of their expressionless quality. No matter what the weather or what her other toilet, she always wore a thin little shawl of dingy brick-dust hue about her shoulders. No matter what the occasion or what the day, she always carried her knitting with her, and seldom ceased the incessant twist, twist of the shining steel among the white cotton meshes. She might put down the needles and lace into the spool-box long enough to open oysters, or wrap up fruit and candy, or count out wood and coal into infinitesimal portions, or do her housework; but the knitting was snatched with avidity at the first spare moment, and the worn, white, blue-marked fingers, half enclosed in kid-glove stalls for protection, would writhe and twist in and out again. Little girls just learning to crochet borrowed their patterns from Tony's wife, and it was considered quite a mark of advancement to have her inspect a bit of lace done by eager, chubby fingers. The ladies in larger houses, whose husbands would be millionaires some day, bought her lace, and gave it to their servants for Christmas presents.

As for Tony, when she was slow in opening his oysters or in cooking his red beans and spaghetti, he roared at her, and prefixed picturesque adjectives to her lace, which made her hide it under her apron with a fearsome look in her dull eyes.

He hated her in a lusty, roaring fashion, as a healthy beefy boy hates a sick cat and torments it to madness. When she displeased him, he beat her, and knocked her frail form on the floor. The children could tell when this had happened. Her eyes would be red, and there would be blue marks on her face and neck. "Poor Mrs. Tony," they would say, and nestle close to her. Tony did not roar at her for petting them, perhaps, because they spent money on the multi-hued candy in glass jars on the shelves.

Her mother appeared upon the scene once, and stayed a short time, but Tony got drunk one day and beat her because she ate too much, and she disappeared soon after. Whence she came and where she departed, no one could tell, not even Mrs. Murphy, the Pauline Pry and Gazette of the block.

Tony had gout, and suffered for many days in roaring helplessness, the while his foot, bound and swathed in many folds of red flannel, lay on the chair before him. In proportion as his gout increased and he bawled from pure physical discomfort, she became light-hearted, and moved about the shop with real, brisk cheeriness. He could not hit her then without such pain that after one or two trials he gave up.

So the dull years had passed, and life had gone on pretty much the same for Tony and the German wife and the shop. The children came on Sunday evenings to buy the stick candy, and on week-days for coal and wood. The servants came to buy oysters for the larger houses, and to gossip over the counter about their employers. The little dry woman knitted, and the big man moved lazily in and out in his red flannel shirt, exchanged politics with the tailor next door through the window, or lounged into Mrs. Murphy's bar and drank fiercely. Some of the children grew up and moved away, and other little girls came to buy candy and eat pink lagniappe fishes, and the shop still thrived.

One day Tony was ill, more than the mummied foot of gout, or the wheeze of asthma; he must keep his bed and send for the doctor.

She clutched his arm when he came, and pulled him into the tiny room.

"Is it anything much, doctor?" she gasped.

Esculapius shook his head as wisely as the occasion would permit. She followed him out of the room into the shop.

"Will he get well, doctor?"

Esculapius buttoned up his frock coat, smoothed

his shining hat, cleared his throat, then replied oracularly, "Madam, he is completely burned

out inside. Empty as a shell, madam, empty as a shell. He cannot live, for he has nothing to live on."

As the cobblestones rattled under the doctor's equipage rolling leisurely up Prytania Street, Tony's wife sat in her chair and laughed with a hearty joyousness that lifted the film from the dull eyes and disclosed a sparkle beneath.

The drear days went by, and Tony lay like a veritable Samson shorn of his strength, for his voice was sunken tO a hoarse, sibilant whisper, and his black eyes gazed fiercely from the shock of hair and beard about a white face. Life went on pretty much as before in the shop. The children paused to ask how, Mr. Tony was, and even hushed the jingles on their bell hoops as they passed the door. Red-headed Jimmie, Mrs. Murphy's nephew, did the hard jobs, such as splitting wood and lifting coal from the bin, and in the intervals between tending the fallen giant and waiting on the customers, Tony's wife sat in her accustomed chair, knitting fiercely, with an inscrutable smile about her purple compressed mouth.

Then John came, introducing himself, serpent-wise, into the Eden of her bosom.

John was Tony's brother, huge and bluff too, but fair and blond, with the beauty of Northern Italy. With the same lack of race pride which Tony had displayed in selecting his German spouse, John had taken unto himself Betty, a daughter of Erin, aggressive, powerful, and cross-eyed. He turned up now, having heard of this illness, and assumed an air of remarkable authority at once.

A hunted look stole into the dull eyes, and after John had departed with blustering directions as to Tony's welfare, she crept to his bedside timidly.

"Tony," she said, "Tony, you are very sick."

An inarticulate growl was the only response.

"Tony, you ought to see the priest, you mustn't go any longer without taking the sacrament."

The growl deepened into words.

"Don't want any priest. You're always after some snivelling old woman's fuss. You and Mrs. Murphy go on with your church, it won't make you any better."

She shivered under this parting shot, and crept back into the shop. Still the priest came next day.

She followed him in to the bedside and knelt timidly.

"Tony," she whispered, "here's Father Leblanc."

Tony was too languid to curse out loud. He only expressed his hate in a toss of the black beard and shaggy mane.

"Tony," she said nervously, " won't you do it now? It won't take long, and it will be better for you when you go. Oh, Tony, don't laugh. Please, Tony, here's the priest."

But the Titan roared aloud: "No, get out. Think I'm a-going to give you a chance to grab my money now? Let me die and go to hell in peace."

Father Leblanc knelt meekly and prayed, and the woman's weak pleadings continued.

"Tony, I've been true and good and faithful to you. Don't die and leave me no better than before. Tony, I do want to be a good woman once, a real-for-true married woman. Tony, here's the priest, say yes."

And she wrung her ringless hands.

"You want my money," said Tony, slowly, "and you shan't have it, not a cent. John shall have it."

Father Leblanc shrank away like a fading spectre. He came next day and next day, only to see re-enacted the same piteous scene: the woman pleading to be made a wife before death hushed Tony's blasphemies, the man chuckling in pain-racked glee at the prospect of her bereaved misery. Not all the prayers of Father Leblanc nor the wailings of Mrs. Murphy could alter the determination of the will beneath the shock of hair. He gloated in his physical weakness at the tenacious grasp on his mentality.

"Tony," she wailed on the last day, her voice rising to a shriek in its eagerness, "tell them I'm your wife, it'll be the same. Only say it, Tony, before you die."

He raised his head, and turned stiff eyes and gibbering mouth on her. Then, with one chill finger pointing at John, fell back dully and heavily.

They buried him with many honours by the Society of Italia's Sons. John took possession of the shop when they returned home, and found the money hidden in the chimney corner.

As for Tony's wife, since she was not his wife after all, they sent her forth in the world penniless, her worn fingers clutching her bundle of clothes in nervous agitation, as though they regretted the time lost from knitting.

VIOLETS

"She tied violets with a tress of her brown hair."

She sat in the yellow glow of the lamplight softly humming these words. It was Easter evening, and newly-risen spring was slowly sinking to a gentle, rosy, opalescent slumber, sweetly tired of the joy which had pervaded it all day. In the dawn of the perfect morn, it had arisen, stretched out its arms to greet the Saviour and said its hallelujahs. Now the evening had come. There was a letter on the table:

Dear, I send you these flowers as my Easter token. Violets, you know are my favorite flowers. They seem always as if about to whisper a love word, and then they signify that thought which passes always between you and me. The orange blossoms — you know their meaning; the little pinks are the flowers you love, the evergreen leaf is the symbol of the endurance of our affection, the tube roses I put in, because once when you kissed and pressed me close in your arms, I had a bunch of tube roses on my bosom, and the heavy fragrance of their crushed loveliness has always lived in my memory. The violets and pinks are from a bunch I wore today, and when kneeling at the altar, during communion, did I sin, dear, when I thought of you? You always wished for a lock of my hair, so I'll tie these flowers with them. Let me wrap them with a bit of ribbon, pale blue, from that little dress I wore last winter to the dance, when we had such a long sweet talk in that forgotten nook. You always loved that dress, it fell in such soft ruffles away from the throat and bosom. You called me your little forget-me-not, that night. I laid the flowers away for a while in our favorite book (Byron) just at the poem we loved best, and now I send them to you. Keep them always in remembrance of me, and if aught should occur to separate us, press these flowers to your lips, and I will be with you in spirit, permeating your heart with unutterable love and happiness.

It is Easter again. As of old, the joyous bells clang out the glad news of the resurrection. The giddy, dancing sunbeams laugh riotously in field and street; birds carol their sweet twitterings everywhere, and the heavy perfume of flowers scents the golden atmosphere with inspiring fragrance. One long, golden sunbeam steals silently into the white-curtained window of a quiet room, and lay on a sleeping face. Cold, pale, still. Its fair young face pressed against the satin-lined casket. Slender, white fingers, idle now, they that had never known rest, locked softly over a bunch of violets; violets and tube roses in her soft, brown hair, violets in the bosom of her long white gown; violets and tube roses and orange blossoms everywhere, until the air was filled with the ascending souls of the human flowers. Some whispered that a broken heart had ceased to flutter in that still, young form, and that it was a mercy for the soul to ascend on the slender sunbeam. Today she kneels at the throne of heaven, where one year ago she had communed at an earthly altar.

Far away in a distant city, a man, carelessly looking among some papers, turned over a faded bunch of flowers tied with a blue ribbon and a lock of hair. He paused meditatively a while, then turning to the woman lounging before the fire, he asked:

"Wife, did you ever send me these?"

She raised her great, black eyes to his with a gesture of ineffable disdain, and replied languidly:

"You know very well I can't bear flowers. How could I ever send such sentimental trash to anyone? Throw them into the fire."

And the Easter bells chimed a solemn requiem as the flames slowly licked up the faded violets. Was it merely fancy on the wife's part, or did the husband really sigh a long, quivering breath of remembrance?

THE WOMAN

The literary manager of the club arose, cleared his throat, adjusted his cravat, fixed his eyes sternly upon the young man and, in a sonorous voice, a little marred by his habitual lisp, asked: "Will you please tell us your opinion upon the question, whether woman's chances for matrimony are increased or decreased when she becomes man's equal as a wage earner?"

The secretary adjusted her eye-glass, and held her pencil alertly poised above her book, ready to note which side the young man took.

He fidgeted, pulled himself together with a violent jerk, and finally spoke his mind.

Someone else did likewise, also someone else, then the women interposed, and jumped on the men, the men retaliated, a wordy war ensued, and the whole matter ended by nothing being decided, pro or con.

Moi? Well, I sawed wood and said nothing, but all the while there was forming in my mind, no, I wouldn't say forming, it was there already. It was this: Why should we salaried women marry? Take the average working woman of today. She works from five to ten hours a day, sometimes doing extra night work. Her work over, she goes home or to her boarding house, as the case may be. Her meals are prepared for her, she has no household cares upon her shoulders, no troublesome dinners to prepare for a fault-finding husband, no fretful children to try her patience, no petty bread and meat economies to adjust. She has her cares, her money troubles, her debts, and her scrimpings, it is true, but they only make her independent, instead of reducing her to a dead level of despair. Her day's work ends at the office, school, factory or store. The rest of the time is hers, undisturbed by the restless going to and fro of housewifely cares, and she can employ it in mental or social diversions. She does not incessantly rely upon the whims of a cross man to take her to such amusements as she desires. In this nineteenth century she is free to go where she pleases without comment, provided it be in a moral atmosphere. Theatres, concerts, lectures, and the lighter amusements of social affairs among her associates, are open to her, and there she can go, see, and be seen, admire and be admired, enjoy and be enjoyed, without a single harrowing thought of the baby's milk or the husband's coffee.

Her earnings are her own, indisputably,

unreservedly, undividedly. She knows to a certainty just how much she can spend, how well she can dress, how far her earnings will go. If there is a dress, a book, a bit of music, a bunch of flowers, or a bit of furniture that she wants, she can get it, and there is no need of asking anyone's advice, or gently hinting Mrs. So and So has a lovely new hat, and there is one ever so much prettier and cheaper downtown. To an independent spirit there is a certain sense of humiliation and wounded pride in asking for money, be it five cents or five hundred dollars. The working woman knows no such pang. She has but to question her account and all is over. In the summer she takes her savings of the winter, packs her trunk and takes a trip more or less extensive, and there is none to say her nay, nothing to bother her save the accumulation of her own baggage. There is an independent, happy, free and easy swing about the motion of her life. Her mind is constantly being broadened by contact with the world in its working clothes; in her leisure moments by the better thoughts of dead and living men which she meets in her applications to books and periodicals; in her vacations, by her studies of nature, or it may be other communities than her own. The freedom which she enjoys she does not trespass upon, for if she did not learn at school she has acquired since habits of strong self-reliance, self-support, earnest thinking, deep discriminations, and firmly believes that the most perfect liberty is that state in which humanity conforms itself to and obeys strictly, without deviation, those laws which are best fitted for their mutual self-advancement.

And so your independent working woman of today comes as near being ideal in her equable self poise as can be imagined. So why should she hasten to give this liberty up in exchange for a serfdom, sweet sometimes, it is true, but which too often becomes galling and unendurable.

It is not marriage that I decry, for I don't think any really sane person would do this. But it is this wholesale marrying of girls in their teens, this rushing into an unknown plane of life to avoid work. Avoid work! What housewife dares call a moment her own?

Marriages might be made in Heaven, but too often they are consummated right here on earth, based on a desire to possess the physical attractions of the woman by the man, pretty much as a child desires a toy, and an innate love of man, a wild desire not to be ridiculed by the foolish as an "old maid," and a

certain delicate shrinking from the work of the world
— laziness is a good name for it — by the woman.
The attraction of mind to mind, the ability of one to
compliment the lights and shadows in the other, the
capacity of either to fulfil the duties of wife or
husband — these do not enter into the contract. That
is why we have divorce courts.

And so our independent woman in every year of
her full, rich, well-rounded life, gaining fresh
knowledge and experience, learning humanity, and
particularly that portion of it which is the other
gender, so well as to avoid clay-footed idols, and
finally when she does consent to bear the yoke upon
her shoulders, does so with perhaps less romance and
glamor than her younger scoffing sisters, but with an
assurance of solid and more lasting happiness. Why
should she have hastened this? Was anything lost by
the delay?

They say that men don't admire this type of
woman, that they prefer the soft, dainty, winning,
mindless creature who cuddles into men's arms,
agrees to everything they say, and looks upon them
as a race of gods turned loose upon this earth for the
edification of womankind. Well, maybe so, but there
is one thing positive, they certainly respect the

independent one, and admire her, too, even if it is at a distance, and that in itself is something. As to the other part, no matter how sensible a woman is on other questions, when she falls in love she is fool enough to believe her adored one a veritable Solomon. Cuddling? Well, she may preside over conventions, brandish her umbrella at board meetings, tramp the streets soliciting subscriptions, wield the blue pencil in an editorial sanctum, hammer a type-writer, smear her nose with ink from a galley full of pied type, lead infant ideas through the tortuous mazes of c-a-t and r-a-t, plead at the bar, or wield the scalpel in a dissecting room, yet when the right moment comes, she will sink as gracefully into his manly embrace, throw her arms as lovingly around his neck, and cuddle as warmly and sweetly to his bosom as her little sister who has done nothing else but think, dream, and practice for that hour. It comes natural, you see.

TEN MINUTES' MUSING

There was a terrible noise in the schoolyard at intermission. Peeping out the windows the boys could be seen huddled in an immense bunch, in the middle of the yard. It looked like a fight, a mob, a knock-down, so we rushed out to the door hastily, fearfully, ready to scold, punish, console, frown, bind up broken heads or drag wounded forms from the melee as the case might be. Nearly every boy in the school was in that seething, swarming mass, and those who weren't were standing around on the edges, screaming and throwing up their hats in hilarious excitement. It was a mob, a fearful mob, but a mob apparently with a vigorous and well-defined purpose. It was a mob that screamed and howled, and kicked, and yelled, and shouted, and perspired, and squirmed, and wriggled, and pushed, and threatened, and poured itself all seemingly upon some central object. It was a mob that had an aim, that was determined to accomplish that aim, even though the whole azure expanse of sky fell upon them. It was a mob with set muscles, straining like whip-cords, eyes on that central object and with heads inward and sturdy legs outward, like prairie horses reversed in a battle. The cheerers and hat throwers on the outside were mirthful, but the mob was not. It howled. Some fell and were trampled over, some weaker ones were even tossed in the air, but the mob never deigned to trouble itself about such trivialities. It was an interesting, nervous whole, with divers parts of separate vitality.

In alarm I looked about for the principal. He was standing at a safe distance with his hands in his pockets watching the seething mass with a broad smile. At sight of my perplexed expression someone was about to venture an explanation, when there was a wild yell, a sudden vehement disintegration of the mass, a mighty rush and clutch at a dark object bobbing in the air. The mist cleared from my intellect as I realized it all — football.

Did you ever stop to see the analogy between a game of football and the interesting little game called life which we play every day? There is one, farfetched as it may seem, though, for that matter, life's game, being one of desperate chances and strategic moves, is analogous to anything.

But, if we could get out of ourselves and soar above the world, far enough to view the Mass beneath in its daily struggles, and near enough the hearts of the people to feel the throbs beneath their boldly carried exteriors, the whole would seem naught but such a maddening rush and senseless-looking crushing. "We are but children of a larger growth," after all, and our ceaseless pursuing after the baubles of this earth are but the struggles for precedence in the business playground.

The football is money. See how the mass rushes after it. Everyone so intent upon his pursuit until all else dwindles into a ridiculous nonentity. The weaker ones go down in the mad pursuit, and are unmercifully trampled upon, but no matter, what is the difference if the foremost win the coveted prize and carry it off. See the big boy in front, he with iron grip, and determined, compressed lips? That boy is a type of the big, merciless man, the Gradgrind of the latter century. His face is set towards the ball, and even though he may crush a dozen small boys, he'll make his way through the mob and come out triumphant. And he'll be the victor longer than anyone else, in spite of the envy and fighting and pushing about him.

To an observer, alike unintelligent about the rules of a foot-ball game, and the conditions which govern the barter and exchange and fluctuations of the world's money market, there is as much difference between the sight of a mass of boys on a play-ground losing their equilibrium over a spheroid of rubber and a mass of men losing their coolness and temper and mental and nervous balance on change as there is between a pine sapling and a mighty forest king — merely a difference of age. The mighty, seething, intensely concentrated mass in its emphatic tendency to one point is the same, in the utter disregard of mental and physical welfare. The momentary triumphs of transitory possessions impress a casual looker-on with the same fearful idea that the human race, after all, is savage to the core, and cultivates its savagery in an inflated happiness at its own nearness to perfection.

But the bell clangs sharply, the overheated, nervous, tingling boys fall into line, and the sudden transition from massing disorder to military precision cuts short the ten minutes' musing.

TITEE

It was cold that day; the great sharp north wind swept out Elysian Fields Street in blasts that made men shiver, and bent everything in its track. The skies hung lowering and gloomy; the usually quiet street was more than deserted, it was dismal.

Titee leaned against one of the brown freight cars for protection against the shrill wind, and warmed his little chapped hands at a blaze of chips and dry grass. "Maybe it'll snow," he muttered, casting a glance at the sky that would have done credit to a practised seaman. Then won't I have fun. Ugh, but the wind blows."

It was Saturday — or Titee would have been in school — the big yellow school on Marigny Street, where he went every day when its bell boomed nine o'clock. Went with a rue and a joyous whoop — presumably to imbibe knowledge, ostensibly to make his teacher's life a burden.

Idle, lazy, dirty, troublesome boy, she called him, to herself, as day by day wore on. and Titee improved not, but let his whole class pass him on its way to a higher grade. A practical joke he relished infinitely more than a practical problem, and a good game at pinsticking was far more entertaining than a language lesson. Moreover, he was always hungry, and would eat in school before the half past ten intermission, thereby losing much good play-time for his voracious appetite.

But there was nothing in natural history that Titee didn't know. He could dissect a butterfly or a mosquito-hawk and describe their parts as accurately as a spectacled student with a scalpel and microscope could talk about a cadaver. The entire Third District, with its swamps and canals and commons and railroad sections, and its wondrous, crooked, tortuous streets was as an open book to Titee. There was not a nook or corner that he did not know or could tell of. There was not a bit of gossip among the gamins, little Creole and Spanish fellows, with dark skins and lovely eyes like Spaniels, that Titee could not tell of. He knew just exactly when it was time for crawfish to be plentiful down in the Claiborne and Marigny canals; just when a poor, breadless fellow might get a job in the big boneyard and fertilizing factory out on the railroad track. As for the levee, with its ships and schooners and sailors. Oh, how he could revel among them! The wondrous ships, the pretty little schooners, where the foreign-looking sailors lay on long moon-lit nights, singing gay bar carols to the tinkle of a guitar and mandolin. All these things, and more, could Titee tell of. He had been down to the Gulf, and out on its treacherous waters through Eads Jetties on a fishing smack, with some jolly, brown sailors, and could interest the whole school-room in the talk lessons," if he chose.

Titee shivered as the wind swept round the freight cars. There isn't much warmth in a bit of a jersey coat.

"Wish it was summer," he murmured, casting another sailor's glance at the sky. "Don't believe I like snow, it's too wet and cold." And, with a last parting caress at the little fire he had built for a minute's warmth, he plunged his hands in his pockets, shut his teeth, and started manfully on his mission out the railroad track towards the swamps.

It was late when Titee came home, to such a home as it was, and he had not fulfilled his errand, so his mother beat him, and sent him to bed supperless. A sharp strap stings in cold weather, and long walks in the teeth of a biting wind creates a keen appetite. But if Titee cried himself to sleep that night, he was up bright and early next morning, and had been to early mass, devoutly kneeling on the cold floor, blowing his fingers to keep them warm, and was home almost before the rest of the family was awake.

There was evidently some great matter of business in this young man's mind, for he scarcely ate his breakfast, and had left the table, eagerly cramming the remainder of his meal in his pockets.

"I wonder what he's up to now?" mused his mother as she watched his little form sturdily trudging the track in the face of the wind, his head, with the rimless cap thrust close on the shock of black hair, bent low, his hands thrust deep in the bulging pockets.

"A new snake, perhaps," ventured the father, "he's a queer child."

But the next day Titee was late for school. It was something unusual, for he was always the first on hand to fix some plan of mechanism to make the teacher miserable. She looked reprovingly at him this morning, when he came in during the arithmetic class, his hair all wind-blown, cheeks rosy from a hard fight with the sharp blasts. But he made up for his tardiness by his extreme goodness all day. Just think, Titee didn't even eat in school. A something unparalleled in the .entire history of his school-life.

When the lunch-hour came, and all the yard was a scene of feast and fun, one of the boys found him standing by one of the posts, disconsolately watching a ham sandwich as it rapidly disappeared down the throat of a sturdy, square-headed little fellow.

"Hello, Edgar," he said. "What yer got for lunch?"

"Nothin'," was the mournful reply.

"Ah, why don't yer stop eating in school for a change? Yer don't ever have nothing to eat."

"I didn't eat today," said Titee, blazing up.

"Yer did!"

"I tell you I didn't," and Titee's hard little fist planted a punctuation mark on his comrade's eye.

A fight in the schoolyard! Poor Titee in disgrace again. But in spite of his battered appearance, a severe scolding from the principal, lines to write, and a further punishment from his mother, Titee scarcely remained for his dinner, but was off, down the railroad track, with his pockets partly stuffed with the remnants of his scanty meal.

Titee was late again the next day. And the next. And the next, until the teacher in despair sent a nicely printed note to his mother about him, which might have done some good, had not Titee taken great pains to tear it up on his way home.

But one day it rained, whole bucketfuls of water, that poured in torrents from a miserable angry sky.

Too wet a day for bits of boys to be trudging to school, so Titee's mother thought, so kept him home to watch the weather through the window, fretting and fuming, like a regular storm-cloud in miniature.

As the day wore on, and the storm did not abate, his mother had to keep a strong watch upon him, or he would have slipped away.

At last dinner came and went, and the gray soddenness of the skies deepened into the blackness of coming night. Someone called Titee to go to bed, but Titee was nowhere to be found.

Under the beds, in corners and closets, through the yard, and in such impossible places as the soap dish and the waterpitcher even. But he had gone as completely as if he had been spirited away. It was of no use to call up the neighbors. He had never been near their houses, they affirmed, so there was nothing to do but to go to the railroad track, where little Titee had been seen so often trudging in the shrill north wind.

So with lantern and sticks, and his little yellow dog, the rescuing party started out the track. The rain had ceased falling, but the wind blew a tremendous gale, scurrying great, gray clouds over a fierce sky. It was not exactly dark, though in this part of the city, there was neither gas nor electricity, and surely on such a night as this, neither moon nor stars dared show their faces in such a grayness of sky, but a sort of all-diffused luminosity was in the air, as though the sea of atmosphere was charged with an ethereal phosphorescence.

Search as they would, there were no signs of poor little Titee. The soft earth between the railroad ties crumbled beneath their feet without showing any small tracks or foot-prints.

"Let us return," said the big brother, "he can't be here anyway."

"No, no," urged the mother, "I feel that he is. Let's go on."

So on they went, slipping on the wet earth, stumbling over the loose rocks, until a sudden wild yelp from Tiger brought them to a standstill. He had rushed ahead of them, and his voice could be heard in the distance, howling piteously.

With a fresh impetus the little muddy party hurried forward. Tiger's yelps could be heard plainer and plainer, mingled now with a muffled wail, as of someone in pain.

And then, after a while they found a pitiful little heap of wet and sodden rags, lying at the foot of a mound of earth and stones thrown upon the side of the track. It was little Titee with a broken leg, all wet and miserable, and moaning.

They picked him up tenderly, and started to carry him home. But he cried and clung to his mother, and begged not to go.

"He's got fever," wailed his mother."

"No, no, it's my old man. He's hungry, sobbed Titee, holding out a little package. It was the remnants of his dinner wet and rain washed.

"What old man?" asked the big brother.

"My old man, oh,please,please don't go home until I see him, I'm not hurting much, I can go."

So yielding to his whim, they carried him further away, down the sides of the track up to an embankment or levee by the sides of the Marigny canal. Then Titee's brother, suddenly stopping, exclaimed:

"Why, here's a cave, a regular Robinson Crusoe affair."

"It's my old man's cave," cried Titee. "Oh, please go in, maybe he's dead."

There can't be much ceremony in entering a cave, there is but one thing to do, walk in. This they did, and holding high the lantern, beheld a strange sight.

On a bed of straw and paper in one corner lay a withered, wizened. whitebearded old man, with wide eyes staring at the unaccustomed sight. In the corner lay a cow.

"It's my old man," cried Titee, joyfully. "Oh, please, grandpa, I couldn't get here today, it rained all morning, and when I ran away this evening, I slipped down and broke something, and oh, grandpa, I'm so tired, and I'm so afraid you're hungry."

So the secret of Titee's jaunts out the railroad was out. In one of his trips around the swamp-land, he had discovered the old man dying from cold and hunger in the fields. Together they had found this cave, and Titee had gathered the straw and brush that scattered itself over the ground and made the bed. A poor old cow turned adrift by an ungrateful master, had crept in and shared the damp dwelling. And thither Titee had trudged twice a day, carrying his luncheon in the morning, and his dinner in the evening, the sole support of a half-dead cripple.

"There's a crown in Heaven for that child," said the officer to whom the case was referred.

So there was, for we scattered winter roses on his little grave down in old St. Rocque's cemetery. The cold and rain, and the broken leg had told their tale

ANARCHY ALLEY

To the casual observer, the quaint, narrow, little alley that lies in the heart of the city is no more than any other of the numerous divisions of streets in which New Orleans delights. But to the idle wanderer, the four squares of much trodden stones of Exchange Alley, presents all the phases of a Latinized portion of America, a bit of Europe, perhaps, the restless, chafing, anarchistic Europe of today, in the midst of the quieter democratic institution of our republic.

It is Bohemia, pure and simple. Bohemia, in all its stages, from the beer saloon and the cheap book-store, to the cheaper cook shop and uncertain lodging house. There the great American institution, the wondrous monarch whom the country supports — the tramp — basks in superior comfort and contented, unmolested indolence. Idleness and labor, poverty and opulence, the honest, law-abiding working man, and the reckless. restless anarchist, jostle side by side, and brush each other's elbows in terms of equality as they do nowhere else.

On the busiest thoroughfares in the city, between two of the most crowded and conservative of cross-streets, lies this alley of Latinism. One might almost

pass it hurriedly, avoiding the crowds that cluster at
this section of the streets, but upon turning into a
narrow section, stone-paved, the place is entered,
appearing to end one square distant, seeming to bar
itself from the larger buildings by an aimless sort of
iron affair, part railing, part posts. There is a
conservative bookstore at the entrance on one side,
and an even more harmless clothing store on the
other. Then comes a saloon with many blind doors,
behind which are vistas of tables, crowded and
crowded with men drinking beer out of 'globes',
large,: round, moony, common affairs. There is a
dingy, pension-claim office, with cripples and
sorrowful-looking women in black, sitting about on
rickety chairs. Somehow, there is always an
impression with me that the mourning dress and
mournful looks are put on to impress the dispenser
and adjuster. It is wicked, but what can one do if
impressions come?

There are more little shops and nondescript
corners that seem to have no possible mission on
earth and are sadly conscious of their aimlessness.
Then the railing is reached, and the alley instead of
ending has merely given itself an angular twist to the
right, and extends three squares further, to a great,

pale green dome and stately entrance.

With the first stepping across Customhouse street, the place widens architecturally, and the atmosphere, too, seems impregnated with a sort of mental freedom, conducive to dangerous theorizing and broody reflections on the inequality of the classes. The sun shines in a strip in the centre, yellow and elusive, like gold. Someone is rattling a gay galop on a piano somewhere. There is a sound of men's voices in a heated discussion, a long whiff of pipe-smoke trails through the sunlight from the bar. The clink of glasses, the chink of silver, and the high treble of a woman's voice scolding a refractory child, mingle in incongruous melody.

Two-storey houses all along. The lower floor divided into stores. Here a paper store, displaying ten-cent novels of detective stories with impossible cuts, illustrating impossible situations of the plot; dye shops, jewellers, tailors, tinsmiths, and a newspaper office. On the upper floor, balconies, dingy, iron-railed, with sickly box-plants, and decrepit garments airing and being turned and tended by dishevelled, slipshod women. Lodging-houses these, some of them, but one is forced to wonder why do the tenants sun their clothes so often? The lines stretched from posts to posts seem always filled with airing garments. Is it economy? Do the owners of the faded vests and patched coats hide in dusky corners while their only garments are receiving the benefit of Old Sol's cleansing rays? It would be something worth knowing if one could.

Plenty of saloons with pianos and swift-footed waiters, tables and cards, and men, men, men. The famous Three Brothers' Saloon occupies a position about midway the alley, and at its doors, the acme, the culminating point, the superlative degree of unquietude and discontent is reached. It is the headquarters of nearly all the great labor organizations in the city. Behind its doors, swinging as easily between the street and the liquor-fumed halls as the soul swings between right and wrong the disturbed minds of the working-men become clouded, heated, and ready for deeds of violence.

Outside were hundreds of like-excited men with angry discussions and bitter recitals of complaints, the seeds of discord sown some time since, perhaps, sprout afresh, blossom and bear fruits. Is there a strike? Then special minions of the law are detailed to this place, for violence and hatred of employers, insurrection and socialism find here ready followers.

Impromptu mass meetings are common, and law-breaking schemes find their cradle beneath its glittering lights. It is always thronged within and without, a veritable nursery of riot and disorder.

And oh, Bohemia, pipes indolence and beer. The atmosphere is impregnated with it, the dust sifts it into your clothes and hair, the sunlight filters it through your brain, the stray snatches of music now and then beat it rhythmically into y our mind. There are some who work, yes and a few places outside of the saloons that seem to be animated with a business motive. There are even some who push their way briskly through the aimless bodies of men, but then there must be an occasional anomaly to break the monotony if nothing more.

It is so unlike the ordinary world, this bit of Bohemia, that one feels a personal grievance when the marble entrance and green dome become solid architectural facts, standing in all the grim solemnity of the main entrance of the Hotel Royal on St. Louis Street ending, with a sudden return to aristocracy, this stamping ground for anarchy.

A CARNIVAL JANGLE

A merry jangle of bells, a pervading sense of noise
and colors. The streets swarm with humanity in all
shapes, manners, forms — a crush of jesters, maskers,
Jim Crows, clowns, ballet girls and Mephistos,
Indians and monkeys. Laughing, jostling, a mass of
men, women and children. Varied and assorted as
ever a crowd gathered since the days of Babel.

Carnival in New Orleans. A brilliant Tuesday in
February. The buildings are a blazing mass of purple,
yellow, and national flags. The streets sound of wild
music, glittering pageants (and comic ones),
befeathered and belled horses. A madding dream of
color and melody and fantasy gone wild in an
effervescent bubble of beauty that shifts and changes
and passes kaleidoscope-like before the bewildered eye.

A bevy of bright-eyed girls and boys of that
uncertainty of age that hovers between childhood
and maturity, were moving down Canal Street when
there was a sudden jostle with another crowd
meeting them. For a minute there was a deafening
clamor of laughter, cracking of whips, which all
maskers carry, jingle and clatter of carnival bells, and
the masked and unmasked extricated themselves and

moved from each other's paths. But in the confusion a tall Prince of Darkness had whispered to one of the girls in the unmasked crowd: "You'd better come with us, Flo, you're wasting time in that tame gang. Slip off, they'll never miss you. We'll get you a rig, and show you what life is."

And so it happened that when a half hour passed, and the bright-eyed bevy missed Flo and couldn't find her, wisely giving up the search at last, that she, the quietest and most bashful of the lot, was being initiated into the mysteries of 'what life is.'

Down Bourbon, Toulouse and St. Peter Streets there are quaint little old-world places where one may be disguised effectually for a tiny consideration. Thither guided by the shapely Mephisto, and guarded by the team of jockeys and ballet girls, tripped Flo. Into one of the dingiest and most ancient-looking of these disguise shops they stopped.

"A disguise for this demoiselle," announced Mephisto to the woman who met them. She was small and wizened and old, with yellow, flabby jaws and neck like the throat of an alligator, and straight white hair that stood from her head uncannily stiff.

"But the demoiselle wishes to appear a boy," she said, gazing eagerly at Flo's long, slender frame. Her voice was old and thin, like the high quavering of an imperfect tuning fork, and her eyes were sharp as talons in their grasping glance.

"Mademoiselle does not wish such a costume," gruffly responded Mephisto.

"*Ma foi,* there is no other," said the ancient, shrugging her shoulders. "But one is left now, mademoiselle would make a fine troubadour."

"Flo," said Mephisto, "it's a daredevil scheme, try it. No one will ever know it but us, and we'll die before we tell. Besides, we must. It's late, and you couldn't find your crowd."

And that was why you might have seen a Mephisto and a slender troubadour of lovely form, with mandolin flung across his shoulder, followed by a bevy of jockeys and ballet girls, laughing and singing as they swept down Rampart Street.

When the flash and glare and brilliancy of Canal Street have palled upon the tired eye, and it is yet too soon to go home to such a prosaic thing as dinner, and one still wishes for novelty, then it is wise to go in the lower districts. Fantasy and fancy and grotesqueness in the costuming and behavior of the maskers run wild. Such dances and whoops and leaps as these Indians and devils do indulge in, such wild curvetings and great walks. And in the open squares, where whole groups do congregate, it is wonderfully amusing. When, too, there is a ball in every available hall, a delirious ball, where one may dance all day for ten cents; dance and grow mad for joy and never know who were your companions, and be yourself unknown. And in the exhilaration of the day, one walks miles and miles, and dances and curvets, and the fatigue is never felt.

In Washington Square, away down where Royal Street empties its stream of children and men into the broad channel of Elysian Fields Avenue, there was a perfect Indian dance. With a little imagination one might have willed away the vision of the surrounding houses and fancied one's self again in the forest, where the natives were holding a sacred riot. The square was filled with spectators, masked and unmasked. It was amusing to watch these mimic 'red men', they seemed so fierce and earnest.

Suddenly one chief touched another on the elbow.

"See that Mephisto and troubadour over there?" he whispered huskily.

"Yes, who are they?"

"I don't know the devil," responded the other quietly, "but I'd know that other form anywhere. It's

Leon, see? I know those white hands like a woman's and that restless head. Ha!"

"But there may be a mistake."

"No. I'd know that one anywhere. I feel it's him. I'll pay him now. Ah, sweetheart, you've waited long, but you shall feast now."

He was caressing something long, and lithe, and glittering beneath his blanket.

In a masked dance it is easy to give a death-blow between the shoulders. Two crowds meet and laugh and shout and mingle almost inextricably, and if a shriek of pain should arise, it is not noticed in the din, and when they part, if one should stagger and fall bleeding to the ground, who can tell who has given the blow? There is naught but an unknown stiletto on the ground, the crowd has dispersed, and masks tell no tales anyway. There is murder, but by whom? For what? *Quien sabe?*

And that is how it happened on Carnival night, in the last mad moments of Rex's reign, a broken-hearted woman sat gazing wide-eyed and mute at a horrible something that lay across the bed. Outside the long sweet march music of many bands floated in mockery and the flash of rockets and Bengal lights illumined the dead white face of the girl troubadour.

THE MAIDEN'S DREAM

The maid had been reading love poetry, where the world lay bathed in moon-light, fragrant with dew-wet roses and jasmine, harmonious with the clear tinkle of mandolin and guitar. Then a lethargy, like unto that which steeps the senses, and benumbs the faculties of the lotus-eaters, enveloped her brain, and she lay as one in a trance — awake, yet sleeping. Conscious, yet unburdened with care.

And there stole into her consciousness, words, thoughts, not of her own, yet she read them not, nor heard them spoken. They fell deep into her heart and soul, softer and more caressing than the overshadowing wing of a mother-dove, sweeter and more thrilling than the last high notes of a violin, and they were these:

Love, most potent, most tyrannical, and most gentle of the passions which sway the human mind, thou art the invisible agency which rules men's souls, which governs men's kingdoms, which controls the universe. By thy mighty will do the silent, eternal hosts of Heaven sweep in sublime procession across the unmeasured blue. The perfect harmony of the spheres is attuned for thee, and by thee; the perfect coloring of the clouds, that which no mortal pigment can dare equal, are thy handiwork. Most ancient of the heathen deities, Eros, powerful God of the Christians, Jehovah, all hail! For a brief possession of thy divine fire have kingdoms waxed and waned, men in all the bitterness of hatred fought, bled, died by millions, their grosser selves to be swept into the bosom of -their ancient mother, an immense holocaust to thee. For thee and thee alone does the world prosper, for thee do men strive to become better than their fellow men; for thee, and through thee have they sunk to such depths of degradation as causes a blush to be painted upon the faces of those that see. All things are subservient to thee. All the delicate intricate workings of that marvellous machine, the human brain, all the passions and desires of the human heart — ambition, desire, greed, hatred, envy, jealousy, all others. Thou breedst them all, O love, thou art all-potent, all-wise, infinite, eternal. Thy power is felt by mortals in all ages, all climes, all conditions. Behold!

A picture came into the maiden's eye: a broad and fertile plain, tender verdure, soft blue sky overhead, with white billowy clouds nearing the horizon like great airy, snow-capped mountains. The soft warm breeze from the south whispered faintly through the tall, slender palms and sent a thrill of joy through the frisky lambkins, who capered by the sides of their graver dams. And there among the riches of the flock stood Laban, haughty, stern, yet withal a kindly gleam in the glance which rested upon the group about him. Hoary the beard that rested upon his breast, but steady the hand that stretched in blessing. Leah, the tender-eyed, the slighted, is there. And Rachel, young and beautiful and blushing beneath the ardent gaze of her handsome lover.

"And Jacob loved Rachel, and said, I will serve thee seven years for Rachel, thy younger daughter."

How different the next scene. Heaven's wrath burst loose upon a single community. Fire, the red-winged demon with brazen throat wide opened, hangs his brooding wings upon an erstwhile happy city. Hades has climbed through the crater of Vesuvius, and leaps in fiendish waves along the land. Few the souls escaping, and God have mercy upon those who stumble through the blinding darkness, made more torturingly hideous by the intermittent flashes of lurid light. And yet there come three, whom the darkness seems not to deter, nor obstacles impede. Only a blind person, accustomed to constant darkness, and familiarized with these streets could walk that way. Nearer they come, a burst of flames thrown into the inky firmament by impish hands, reveals Glaucus, supporting the half-fainting Ione, following Nydia, frail, blind, flower-loving Nydia, sacrificing life for her unloving beloved.

And then the burning southern sun shone bright and golden over the silken sails of the Nile serpent's ships, glinted on the armor and weapons of the famous galley, shone with a warm caressing touch upon her beauty, as though it loved this queen, as powerful in her sphere as he in his. It is at Actium, and the fate of nations and generations yet unborn hang, as the sword of Damocles hung, upon the tiny thread of destiny. Egypt herself, her splendid barbaric beauty acting like an inspiration upon the craven followers, leads on, foremost in this fierce struggle. Then, the tide turns and, overpowered, they fly before disgrace and defeat. Antony is there. The traitor. Dishonored. False to his country, yet true to his love. Antony, whom ambition could not lure from her passionate caresses. Antony, murmuring softly:

"Egypt, thou knowest too well
My heart was to thy rudder tied by the strings

> *And thou should'st tow me after. Over my spirit*
> *Thy full supremacy thou knewest,*
> *And that thy beck might from the bidding of the gods*
> *Command me."*

Picture after picture flashed through the maiden's mind. Agnes, the gentle, sacrificing, burrowing like some frantic animal through the ruins of Lisbon, saving her lover, Franklin, by teeth and bleeding hands. Dora, the patient, serving a loveless existence, saving her rival from starvation and destitution. The stern, dark, exiled Florentine poet, with that one silver ray in his clouded life — Beatrice.

She heard the piping of an elfish voice, "Mother, why does the minister keep his hands over his heart?" and the white drawn face of Hester Prynne, with her scarlet elf-child, passed slowly across her vision. The wretched misery of deluded Lucius and his mysterious Lamia she saw, and watched with breathless interest the formation of that 'Brotherhood of the Rose.' There was radiant Armorel, from sea-blown, wavewashed Lyonesse, her perfect head poised in loving caress over the magic violin. Dark-eyed Corinne, head drooped gently as she improvised those Famed world symphonies passed, almost before Edna and St. Elmo had crossed the threshold of the church happy in the love now consecrated through her to God. Oh, the pictures, the forms, the love words which crowded her mind. They thrilled her -heart, crushed out all else save a crushing, over-powering sense of perfect, complete joy. A joy that sought to express itself in wondrous melodies and silences, filled with thoughts too deep and sacred for words. Overpowered with the magnificence of his reign, overwhelmed with the complete subjugation of all things unto him, do you wonder that she awoke and placing both hands into those of the lover at her side, whispered:

"Take all of me. I am thine own — heart, soul, brain, body, all. All that I am or dream is thine forever. Yea, though space should teem with thy conditions, I'd fulfil the whole, were to fulfil them to be loved by thee."

THE STONES OF THE VILLAGE

VICTOR GRABERT strode down the one, wide, tree-shaded street of the village, his heart throbbing with a bitterness and anger that seemed too great to bear. So often had he gone home in the same spirit, however, that it had grown nearly second nature to him. This dull, sullen resentment, flaming out now and then into almost murderous vindictiveness. Behind him there floated derisive laughs and shouts, the taunts of little brutes, boys of his own age.

He reached the tumbledown cottage at the farther end of the street and flung himself on the battered step. Grandmère Grabért sat rocking herself to and fro, crooning a bit of song brought over from the West Indies years ago; but when the boy sat silent, his head bowed in his hands, she paused in the midst of a line and regarded him with keen, piercing eyes.

"Eh, Victor?" she asked. That was all, but he understood. He raised his head and waved a hand angrily down the street toward the lighted square that marked the village center.

"Those boys," he gulped.

Grandmère Grabért laid a sympathetic hand on his black curls, but withdrew it the next instant.

"*Bien*," she said angrily. "Why d'you go by dem, eh? Why not keep to yourself? They don't want you, they don't care for you. Ain't you got no sense?"

"Oh, but Grandmère," he wailed piteously, "I want to play."

The old woman stood up in the doorway, her tall, spare form towering menacingly over him.

"You want to play, eh? Why? You don't need no play. Those boys," she swept a magnificent gesture down the street, "they're fools!"

"If I could play with—" began Victor, but his grandmother caught him by the wrist and held him as in a vise.

"Hush," she cried. "You must be goin' crazy."

Still holding him by the wrist, she pulled him indoors.

It was a two-room house, bare and poor and miserable, but never had it seemed so meager before to Victor as it did this night. The supper was frugal almost to the starvation point. They ate in silence, and afterward Victor threw himself on his cot in the corner of the kitchen and closed his eyes. Grandmère Grabért thought him asleep and closed the door noiselessly as she went into her own room. But he was awake, and his mind was like a shifting kaleidoscope of miserable incidents and heartaches. He had lived fourteen years, and he could remember most of them as years of misery. He had never known a mother's love, for his mother had died, so he was told, when he was but a few months old. No one ever spoke to him of a father, and Grandmère Grabért had been all to him. She was kind, after a stern, unloving fashion, and she provided for him as best she could. He had picked up some sort of an education at the parish school. It was a good one after its way, but his life there had been such a succession of miseries that he rebelled one day and refused to go anymore.

His earliest memories were clustered about this poor little cottage. He could see himself toddling about its broken steps, playing alone with a few broken pieces of china which his fancy magnified into glorious toys. He remembered his first whipping too. Tired one day of the loneliness which even the broken china could not mitigate, he had toddled out the side gate after a merry group of little black and yellow boys of his own age. When Grandmère Grabért, missing him from his accustomed garden corner, came to look for him, she found him sitting contentedly in the center of the group in the dusty street, all of them gravely scooping up handfuls of the gravelly dirt and trickling it down their chubby bare legs. Grandmère snatched at him fiercely, and he whimpered, for he was learning for the first time what fear was.

"What you mean?" she hissed at him. "What you mean playing in the street with those niggers?" And she struck at him wildly with her open hand.

He looked up into her brown face surmounted by a wealth of curly black hair faintly streaked with gray, but he was too frightened to question.

It had been loneliness ever since. For the parents of the little black and yellow boys, resenting the insult Grandmère had offered their offspring, sternly bade them have nothing more to do with Victor. Then when he toddled after some other little boys, whose faces were white like his own, they ran him away with derisive hoots of "Nigger! Nigger!" And again, he could not understand.

Hardest of all, though, was when Grandmère sternly bade him cease speaking the soft Creole patois that they chatted together and forced him to learn English. The result was a confused jumble which was no language at all; that when he spoke it in the streets or in the school, all the boys, white and black and yellow, hooted at him and called him

"White nigger! White nigger!"

He writhed on his cot that night and lived over all the anguish of his years until hot tears scalded their way down a burning face, and he fell into a troubled sleep wherein he sobbed over some dreamland miseries.

The next morning, Grandmère eyed his heavy swollen eyes sharply, and a momentary thrill of compassion passed over her and found expression in a new tenderness of manner toward him as she served his breakfast. She had also thought over the matter in the night, and it bore fruit in an unexpected way.

Some few weeks after, Victor found himself timidly ringing the doorbell of a house on Hospital Street in New Orleans. His heart throbbed in painful unison to the jangle of the bell. How was he to know that old Madame Guichard, Grandmère's one friend in the city, to whom she had confided him, would be kind? He had walked from the river landing to the house, timidly inquiring the way of busy pedestrians. He was hungry and frightened. Never in all his life had he seen so many people before, and in all the busy streets there was not one eye which would light up with recognition when it met his own. Moreover, it had been a weary journey down the Red River, thence into the Mississippi, and finally here. Perhaps it had not been devoid of interest, after its fashion, but Victor did not know. He was too heartsick at leaving home.

However, Madame Guichard was kind. She welcomed him with a volubility and overflow of tenderness that acted like balm to the boy's sore spirit. Thence they were firm friends, even confidants.

Victor must find work to do. Grandmère Grabért's idea in sending him to New Orleans was that he might "mek one man of himself," as she phrased it. And Victor, grown suddenly old in the sense that he had a responsibility to bear, set about his search valiantly.

It chanced one day that he saw a sign in an old bookstore on Royal Street that stated in both French and English the need of a boy. Almost before he knew it, he had entered the shop and was gasping out some choked words to the little old man who sat behind the counter.

The old man looked keenly over his glasses at the boy and rubbed his bald head reflectively. In order to do this, he had to take off an old black silk cap, which he looked at with apparent regret.

"Eh, what you say?" he asked sharply, when Victor had finished.

"I want a place to work," stammered the boy again.

"Eh, you do? Well, can you read?"

"Yes sir," replied Victor.

The old man got down from his stool, came from behind the counter, and putting his finger under the boy's chin, stared hard into his eyes. They met his own unflinchingly, though there was the suspicion of pathos and timidity in their brown depths.

"Do you know where you live, eh?"

"On Hospital Street," said Victor. It did not occur to him to give the number, and the old man did not ask.

"*Très bien*," grunted the book seller, and his interest relaxed. He gave a few curt directions about the manner of work Victor was to do and settled himself again upon his stool, poring into his dingy book with renewed ardor.

Thus began Victor's commercial life. It was an easy one. At seven, he opened the shutters of the little shop and swept and dusted. At eight, the book-seller came downstairs and passed out to get his coffee at the restaurant across the street. At eight in the evening, the shop was closed again. That was all.

Occasionally, there came a customer, but not often, for there were only odd books and rare ones in the shop, and those who came were usually old, yellow, querulous bookworms, who nosed about for hours and went away leaving many bank notes behind them. Sometimes there was an errand to do, and sometimes there came a customer when the proprietor was out. It was an easy matter to wait on them. He had but to point to the shelves and say, "Monsieur will be in directly," and all was settled, for those who came here to buy had plenty of leisure and did not mind waiting.

So a year went by, then two and three, and the stream of Victor's life flowed smoothly on its uneventful way. He had grown tall and thin, and often Madame Guichard would look at him and chuckle to herself, "Ha, he is like a beanpole, yes, *mais*—" and there would be a world of unfinished reflection in that last word.

Victor had grown pale from much reading. Like a shadow of the old book-seller he sat day after day poring into some dusty yellow-paged book, and his mind was a queer jumble of ideas. History and philosophy and old-fashioned social economy were tangled with French romance and classic mythology and astrology and mysticism He had made few friends, for his experience in the village had made him wary of strangers. Every week, he wrote to Grandmère Grabért and sent her part of his earnings. In his way he was happy, and if he was lonely, he had ceased to care about it, for his world was peopled with images of his own fancying.

Then all at once, the world he had built about him tumbled down, and he was left, staring helplessly at its ruins. The little book-seller died one day, and his shop and its books were sold by an unscrupulous nephew who cared not for bindings nor precious yellowed pages, but only for the grossly material things that money can buy. Victor ground his teeth as the auctioneer's strident voice sounded through the shop where all once had been hushed quiet, and wept as he saw some of his favorite books carried away by men and women who he was sure could not appreciate their value.

He dried his tears, however, the next day, when a grave-faced lawyer came to the little house on Hospital Street and informed him that he had been left a sum of money by the book-seller.

Victor sat staring at him helplessly. Money meant little to him. He never needed it, never used it. After he had sent Grandmère her sum each week Madame Guichard kept the rest and doled it out to him as he needed it for car fare and clothes.

"The interest of the money," continued the lawyer clearing his throat, "is sufficient to keep you very handsomely without touching the principal. It was my client's wish that you should enter Tulane College and there fit yourself for your profession. He had great confidence in your ability."

"Tulane College!" cried Victor. "Why—"

He stopped suddenly. The hot blood mounted to his face. He glanced furtively about the room. Madame Guichard was not near; the lawyer had seen no one but him. Then why tell him? His heart leaped wildly at the thought. Well, Grandmère would have willed it so.

The lawyer was waiting politely for him to finish his sentence.

"Why, I should have to study in order to enter there," finished Victor lamely.

"Exactly so," said Mr. Buckley, "and as I have, in a way, been appointed your guardian, I will see to that."

Victor found himself murmuring confused thanks and goodbyes to Mr. Buckley. After he had gone, the boy sat down and gazed blankly at the wall. Then he wrote a long letter to Grandmère.

A week later, he changed boarding places at Mr. Buckley's advice and entered a preparatory school for Tulane. And still, Madame Guichard and Mr. Buckley had not met.

It was a handsomely furnished office on Carondelet Street in which Lawyer Grabért sat some years later. His day's work done, he was leaning back in his chair and smiling pleasantly out of the window. Within was warmth and light and cheer; outside, the wind howled and gusty rains beat against the window pane. Lawyer Grabért smiled again as he looked about at the comfort and found himself pitying those who were forced to buffet the storm afoot. He rose finally and, donning his overcoat, called a cab and was driven to his rooms in the most fashionable part of the city. There he found his old-time college friend, awaiting him with some impatience.

"Thought you never were coming, old man," was his greeting.

Grabért smiled pleasantly, "Well, I was a bit tired,

you know," he answered, "and I have been sitting idle for an hour or more, just relaxing, as it were."

Vannier laid his hand affectionately on the other's shoulder. "That was a mighty effort you made today," he said earnestly. "I, for one, am proud of you."

"Thank you," replied Grabért simply, and the two sat silent for a minute.

"Going to the Charles's dance tonight?" asked Vannier finally.

"I don't believe I am. I am tired and lazy."

"It will do you good. Come on."

"No, I want to read and ruminate."

"Ruminate over your good fortune of today?"

"If you will have it so, yes."

But it was not simply over his good fortune of that day over which Grabért pondered. It was over the good fortune of the past fifteen years. From school to college, and from college to law school he had gone, and thence into practice, and he was now accredited a successful young lawyer. His small fortune, which Mr. Buckley, with generous kindness had invested wisely, had almost doubled, and his school career, while not of the brilliant, meteoric kind, had been pleasant and profitable. He had made friends, at first, with the boys he met, and they in turn had taken him into their homes. Now and then, the Buckleys asked him to dinner, and he was seen occasionally in their box at the opera. He was rapidly becoming a social favorite, and girls vied with each other to dance with him. No one had asked any questions, and he had volunteered no information concerning himself. Vannier, who had known him in preparatory school days, had said that he was a young country fellow with some money, no connections, and a ward of Mr. Buckley's and, somehow, contrary to the usual social custom of the South, this meager account had passed muster. But Vannier's family had been a social arbiter for many years, and Grabért's personality was pleasing without being aggressive, so he had passed through the portals of the social world and was in the inner circle.

One year, when he and Vannier were in Switzerland, pretending to climb impossible mountains and in reality smoking many cigars a day on hotel porches, a letter came to Grabért from the priest of his old village, telling him that Grandmère Grabért had been laid away in the parish churchyard. There was no more to tell. The little old hut had been sold to pay funeral expenses.

"Poor Grandmère," sighed Victor. "She did care

for me after her fashion. I'll go take a look at her grave when I go back."

But he did not go, for when he returned to Louisiana, he was too busy, then he decided that it would be useless, sentimental folly. Moreover, he had no love for the old village. Its very name suggested things that made him turn and look about him nervously. He had long since eliminated Madame Guichard from his list of acquaintances.

And yet, as he sat there in his cozy study that night and smiled as he went over in his mind triumph after triumph which he had made since the old bookstore days in Royal Street, he was conscious of a subtle undercurrent of annoyance; a sort of mental reservation that placed itself on every pleasant memory.

"I wonder what's the matter with me?" he asked himself as he rose and paced the floor impatiently. Then he tried to recall his other triumph, the one of the day. The case of Tate vs. Tate, a famous will contest, had been dragging through the courts for seven years, and his speech had decided it that day. He could hear the applause of the courtroom as he sat down, but it rang hollow in his ears, for he remembered another scene. The day before he had been in another court and found himself interested in the prisoner before the bar. The offense was a slight one, a mere technicality. Grabért was conscious of something pleasant in the man's face; a scrupulous neatness in his dress, an unostentatious conforming to the prevailing style. The Recorder, however, was short and brusque.

"Wilson," he growled. "Oh yes, I know you, always kicking up some sort of a row about theater seats and cars. Hhm-hm. What do you mean by coming before me with a flower in your buttonhole?"

The prisoner looked down indifferently at the bud on his coat and made no reply.

"Hey?" growled the Recorder. "You niggers are putting yourselves up too much for me."

At the forbidden word, the blood rushed to Grabért's face, and he started from his seat angrily. The next instant he had recovered himself and buried his face in a paper. After Wilson had paid his fine, Grabért looked at him furtively as he passed out. His face was perfectly impassive, but his eyes flashed defiantly. The lawyer was tingling with rage and indignation, although the affront had not been given him.

"If Recorder Grant had any reason to think that I

was in any way like Wilson, I would stand no better show," he mused bitterly.

However, as he thought it over tonight, he decided that he was a sentimental fool. "What have I to do with them" he asked himself. "I must be careful."

The next week he discharged the man who cared for his office. He was a Negro, and Grabért had no fault to find with him generally, but he found himself with a growing sympathy toward the man, and since the episode in the courtroom, he was morbidly nervous lest something in his manner would betray him. Thereafter, a round-eyed Irish boy cared for his rooms.

The Vanniers were wont to smile indulgently at his every move. Elise Vannier particularly was more than interested in his work. He had a way of dropping in of evenings and talking over his cases and speeches with her in a cozy corner of the library. She had a gracious sympathetic manner that was soothing and a cheery fund of repartee to whet her conversation. Victor found himself drifting into sentimental bits of talk now and then. He found himself carrying around in his pocketbook a faded rose which she had once worn, and when he laughed at it one day and started to throw it in the wastebasket, he suddenly kissed it instead and replaced it in the pocketbook. That Elise was not indifferent to him he could easily see. She had not learned yet how to veil her eyes and mask her face under a cool assumption of superiority. She would give him her hand, when they met, with a girlish impulsiveness, and her color came and went under his gaze. Sometimes, when he held her hand a bit longer than necessary, he could feel it flutter in his own, and she would sigh a quick little gasp that made his heart leap and choked his utterance.

They were tucked away in their usual cozy corner one evening, and the conversation had drifted to the problem of where they would spend the summer.

"Papa wants to go to the country house," pouted Elise, "and Mama and I don't want to go. It isn't fair, of course, because when we go so far away, Papa can be with us only for a few weeks when he can get away from his office, while if we go to the country place, he can run up every few days. But it is so dull there, don't you think so?"

Victor recalled some pleasant vacation days at the plantation home and laughed. "Not if you are there."

"Yes, but you see, I can't take myself for a companion. Now if you'll promise to come up sometimes, it will be better."

"If I may, I shall be delighted to come."

Elise laughed intimately. "If you may," she replied. "As if such a word had to enter into our plans. Oh, but Victor, haven't you some sort of plantation somewhere? It seems to me that I heard Steven years ago speak of your home in the country, and I wondered sometimes that you never spoke of it or ever mentioned having visited it.

The girl's artless words were bringing cold sweat to Victor's brow, his tongue felt heavy and useless, but he managed to answer quietly, "I have no home in the country."

"Well, didn't you ever own one, or your family?"

"It was old quite a good many years ago," he replied, and a vision of the little old hut with its tumbledown steps and weed-grown garden came into his mind.

"Where was it?" pursued Elise innocently.

"Oh, away up in St. Landry parish, too far away from civilization to mention." He tried to laugh, but it was a hollow forced attempt that rang false. But Elise was too absorbed in her own thoughts of the summer to notice.

"And you haven't a relative living?" she continued.

"Not one."

"How strange. Why, it seems to me if I did not have a half a hundred cousins and uncles and aunts that I should feel somehow out of touch with the world."

He did not reply, and she chatted away on another topic.

When he was alone in his room that night, he paced the floor again, chewing wildly at a cigar that he had forgotten to light.

"What did she mean? What did she mean?" he asked himself over and over. Could she have heard or suspected anything that she was trying to find out about? Could any action, any unguarded expression of his, have set the family thinking? But he soon dismissed the thought as unworthy of him. Elise was too frank and transparent a girl to stoop to subterfuge. If she wished to know anything, she was wont to ask out at once, and if she had once thought anyone was sailing under false colors, she would say so frankly and dismiss them from her presence.

Well, he must be prepared to answer questions if he were going to marry her. The family would want to know all about him, and Elise, herself, would be curious for more than her brother Steve Vannier's

meager account. But was he going to marry Elise?
That was the question.

He sat down and buried his head in his hands.
Would it be right for him to take a wife, especially
such a woman as Elise, and from such a family as the
Vanniers? Would it be fair? Would it be just? If they
knew and were willing, it would be different. But
they did not know, and they would not consent if
they did. In fancy, he saw the dainty girl whom he
loved shrinking from him as he told her of
Grandmère Grabért and the village boys. This last
thought made him set his teeth hard, and the hot
blood rushed to his face.

Well, why not, after all, why not? What was the
difference between him and the hosts of other suitors
who hovered about Elise? They had money, so had
he. They had education, polite training, culture,
social position; so had he. But they had family
traditions, and he had none. Most of them could
point to a long line of family portraits with justifiable
pride; while if he had had a picture of Grandmère
Grabért, he would have destroyed it fearfully, lest it
fall into the hands of some too curious person. This
was the subtle barrier that separated them. He
recalled with a sting how often he had had to sit

silent and constrained when the conversation turned to ancestors and family traditions. He might be one with his companions and friends in everything but this. He must ever be on the outside, hovering at the gates, as it were. Into the inner life of his social world, he might never enter. The charming impoliteness of an intercourse begun by their fathers and grandfathers was not for him. There must always be a certain formality with him, even though they were his most intimate friends. He had not fifty cousins, therefore, as Elise phrased it, he was "out of touch with the world."

"If ever I have a son or a daughter," he found himself saying unconsciously, "I would try to save him from this."

Then he laughed bitterly as he realized the irony of the thought. Well, anyway, Elise loved him. There was a sweet consolation in that. He had but to look into her frank eyes and read her soul. Perhaps she wondered why he had not spoken. Should he speak? There he was back at the old question again.

"According to the standard of the world," he mused reflectively, "my blood is tainted in two ways. Who knows it? No one but myself, and I shall not tell. Otherwise, I am quite as good as the rest, and Elise loves me."

But even this thought failed of its sweetness in a moment. Elise loved him because she did not know. He found a sickening anger and disgust rising in himself at a people whose prejudices made him live a life of deception. He would cater to their traditions no longer; he would be honest. Then he found himself shrinking from the alternative with a dread that made him wonder. It was the old problem of his life in the village; and the boys, both white and black and yellow, stood as before, with stones in their hands to hurl at him.

He went to bed worn out with the struggle, but still with no definite idea what to do. Sleep was impossible. He rolled and tossed miserably and cursed the fate that had thrown him in such a position. He had never thought very seriously over the subject before. He had rather drifted with the tide and accepted what came to him as a sort of recompense the world owed him for his unhappy childhood. He had known fear, yes, and qualms now and then, and a hot resentment occasionally when the outsideness of his situation was inborn to him; but that was all. Elise had awakened a disagreeable conscientiousness within him, which he decided was as unpleasant as it was unnecessary.

He could not sleep, so he arose, and dressing, walked out and stood on the banquette. The low hum of the city came to him like the droning of some sleepy insect, and ever and anon, the quick flash and fire of the gas houses like a huge winking fiery eye lit up the south of the city. It was inexpressingly soothing to Victor; the great unknowing city, teeming with life and with lives whose sadness mocked his own teacup tempest. He smiled and shook himself as a dog shakes off the water from his coat.

"I think a walk will help me out;" he said absently, and presently he was striding down St. Charles Avenue, around Lee Circle and down to Canal Street, where the lights and glare absorbed him for a while. He walked out the wide boulevard toward Claiborne Street, hardly thinking, hardly realizing that he was walking. When he was thoroughly worn out, he retraced his steps and dropped wearily into a restaurant near Bourbon Street.

"Hello!" said a familiar voice from a table as he entered. Victor turned and recognized Frank Ward, a little oculist, whose office was in the same building as his own.

"Another night owl besides myself," laughed

Ward, making room for him at his table. "Can't you sleep too, old fellow?"

"Not very well," said Victor taking the proferred seat. "I believe I'm getting nerves. Think I need toning up."

"Well, you'd have been toned up if you had been in here a few minutes ago. Why—why—" and Ward went off into peals of laughter at the memory of the scene.

"What was it?" asked Victor.

"A fellow came in here, nice sort of fellow, apparently, and wanted to have supper. Well, would you believe it, when they wouldn't serve him, he wanted to fight everything in sight. It was positively exciting for a time."

"Why wouldn't the waiter serve him?" Victor tried to make his tone indifferent, but he felt the quaver in his voice.

"Why? Why, he was a darkey, you know."

"Well, what of it?" demanded Grabért fiercely. "Wasn't he quiet, well-dressed, polite? Didn't he have money?"

"My dear fellow," began Ward mockingly. "Upon my word, I believe you are losing your mind. You do need toning up or something. Would you, could you?"

"Oh pshaw," broke in Grabért. "I believe I am losing my mind. Really, Ward, I need something to make me sleep. My head aches."

Ward was at once all sympathy and advice, and chiding to the waiter for his slowness in filling their order. Victor toyed with his food and made an excuse to leave the restaurant as soon as he could decently.

"Good heavens," he said when he was alone. "What will I do next?" His outburst of indignation at Ward's narrative had come from his lips almost before he knew it, and he was frightened, frightened at his own unguardedness. He did not know what had come over him.

"I must be careful, I must be careful," he muttered to himself. "I must go to the other extreme, if necessary." He was pacing his rooms again, and suddenly, he faced the mirror.

"You wouldn't fare any better than the rest, if they knew," he told the reflection. "You poor wretch, what are you?"

When he thought of Elise, he smiled. He loved her, but he hated the traditions which she represented. He was conscious of a blind fury which bade him wreak vengeance on those traditions, and of a cowardly fear which cried out to him to retain his position in the world's and Elise's eyes at any cost.

Mrs. Grabért was delighted to have visiting her her old school friend from Virginia, and the two spent hours laughing over their girlish escapades, and comparing notes about their little ones. Each was confident that her darling had said the cutest things, and their polite deference to each other's opinions on the matter was a sham through which each saw without resentment.

"But Elise," remonstrated Mrs. Allen, "I think it so strange you don't have a mammy for Baby Vannier. He would be so much better cared for than by that harumscarum young white girl you have."

"I think so too, Adelaide," sighed Mrs. Grabért. "It seems strange for me not to have a darkey maid about, but Victor can't bear them. I cried and cried for my old mammy, but he was stern. He doesn't like darkeys, you know, and he says old mammies just frighten children and ruin their childhood. I don't see how he could say that, do you?" She looked wistfully to Mrs. Allen for sympathy.

"I don't know," mused that lady. "We were all looked after by our mammies, and I think they are the best kind of nurses."

"And Victor won't have any kind of darkey servant either here or at the office. He says they're shiftless and worthless and generally no-account. Of course, he knows, he's had lots of experience with them in his business."

Mrs. Allen folded her hands behind her head and stared hard at the ceiling. "Oh well, men don't know everything," she said, "and Victor may come around to our way of thinking after all."

It was late that evening when the lawyer came in for dinner. His eyes had acquired a habit of veiling themselves under their lashes as if they were constantly concealing something which they feared might be wrenched from them by a stare. He was nervous and restless, with a habit of glancing about him furtively, and a twitching compressing of his lips when he had finished a sentence, which somehow reminded you of a kind-hearted judge who is forced to give a death sentence.

Elise met him at the door as was her wont, and she knew from the first glance into his eyes that something had disturbed him more than usual that day, but she forbore asking questions, for she knew he would tell her when the time had come.

They were in their room that night when the rest of the household lay in slumber. He sat for a long while gazing at the open fire, then he passed his hand over his forehead wearily.

"I have had a rather unpleasant experience today," he began.

"Yes."

"Pavageau, again."

His wife was brushing her hair before the mirror. At the name she turned hastily with the brush in her uplifted hand.

"I can't understand, Victor, why you must have dealings with that man. He is constantly irritating you. I simply wouldn't associate with him."

"I don't," and he laughed at her feminine argument. It isn't a question of association, *chérie*, it's a purely business and unsocial relation, if relation it may be called, that throws us together."

She threw down the brush petulantly and came to his side. "Victor," she began hesitatingly, her arms about his neck, her face close to his, "won't you give up politics for me? It was ever so much nicer when you were just a lawyer and wanted only to be the best lawyer in the state, without all this worry about corruption and votes and such things. You've changed, oh Victor, you've changed so. Baby and I won't know you after a while."

He put her gently on his knee. "You mustn't blame the poor politics, darling. Don't you think, perhaps, it's the inevitable hardening and embittering that must come to us all as we grow older?"

"No, I don't," she replied emphatically. "Why do you go into this struggle, anyhow? You have nothing to gain but an empty honor. It won't bring you more money, or make you more loved or respected. Why must you be mixed up with such awful people?"

"I don't know," he said wearily.

And in truth, he did not know. He had gone on after his marriage with Elise making one success after another. It seemed that a beneficent Providence had singled him out as the one man in the state upon whom to heap the most lavish attentions. He was popular after the fashion of those who are high in the esteem of the world; and this very fact made him tremble the more, for he feared that should some disclosure come, he could not stand the shock of public opinion that must overwhelm him.

"What disclosure?" he would say impatiently when such a thought would come to him. "Where could it come from, and then, what is there to disclose?"

Thus he would deceive himself for as much as a month at a time.

He was surprised to find awaiting him in his office one day the man Wilson, whom he remembered in the courtroom before Recorder Grant. He was surprised and annoyed. Why had the man come to his office? Had he seen the tell-tale flush on his face that day?

But it was soon evident that Wilson did not even remember having seen him before.

"I came to see if I could retain you in a case of mine," he began, after the usual formalities of greeting were over.

"I am afraid, my good man," said Grabért brusquely, "that you have mistaken the office."

Wilson's face flushed at the appellation, but he went on bravely. I have not mistaken the office. I know you are the best civil lawyer in the city, and I want your services."

"An impossible thing."

"Why? Are you too busy? My case is a simple thing, a mere point in law, but I want the best authority and the best opinion brought to bear on it."

"I could not give you any help and, I fear, we do

not understand each other. I do not wish to."

He turned to his desk abruptly.

"What could he have meant by coming to me?" he questioned himself fearfully, as Wilson left the office. "Do I look like a man likely to take up his impossible contentions?"

He did not look like it, nor was he. When it came to a question involving the negro, Victor Grabért was noted for his stern, unrelenting attitude; it was simply impossible to convince him that there was anything but sheerest incapacity in that race. For him, no good could come out of this Nazareth. He was liked and respected by men of his political belief because, even when he was a candidate for a judgeship, neither money nor the possible chance of a deluge of votes from the First and Fourth Wards could cause him to swerve one hair's breadth from his opinion of the black inhabitants of those wards.

Pavageau, however, was his *bête noir*. Pavageau was a lawyer, a cool-headed, calculating man with steely eyes set in a grim brown face. They had first met in the courtroom in a case which involved the question whether a man may set aside the will of his father who, disregarding the legal offspring of another race than himself, chooses to leave his property to educational institutions which would not have granted admission to that son. Pavageau represented the son. He lost, of course. The judge, the jury, the people, and Grabért were against him; but he fought his fight with a grim determination which commanded Victor's admiration and respect.

"Fools," he said between his teeth to himself, when they were crowding about him with congratulations. "Fools, can't they see who is the abler man of the two?"

He wanted to go up to Pavageau and give him his hand; to tell him that he was proud of him and that he had really won the case, but public opinion was against him; but he dared not. Another one of his colleagues might; but he was afraid. Pavageau and the world might misunderstand, or would it be understanding?

Thereafter they met often. Either by some freak of nature, or because there was a shrewd sense of the possibilities in his position, Pavageau was of the same political side of the fence as Grabért. Secretly, he admired the man; he respected him; he liked him, and because of this he was always ready with sneer and invective for him. He fought him bitterly when there was no occasion for fighting, and Pavageau became his enemy, and his name a very synonym of horror to Elise, who learned to trace her husband's fits of moodiness and depression to the one source.

Meanwhile, Vannier Grabért was growing up, a handsome lad, with his father's and mother's physical beauty, and a strength and force of character that belonged to neither. In him, Grabért saw the reparation of all his childhood's wrongs and sufferings. The boy realized all his own longings. He had family traditions, and a social position which was his from birth and an inalienable right to hold up his head without an unknown fear gripping at his heart. Grabért felt that he could forgive all the village boys of long ago, and the imaginary village boys of today when he looked at his son. He had bought and paid for Vannier's freedom and happiness. The coins may have been each a drop of his heart's blood, but he had reckoned the cost before he had given it.

It was a source of great pride for him to take the boy to court with him, now that he was a judge, and one Saturday morning when he was starting out, Vannier asked if he might go.

"There is nothing that would interest you today, *mon fils*," he said tenderly, "but you may go."

In fact, there was nothing interesting that day;

merely a troublesome old woman, who instead of taking her fair-skinned grandchild out of the school, where it had been found it did not belong, had preferred to bring the matter to court. She was represented by Pavageau. Of course, there was not the ghost of a show for her. Pavageau had told her that. The law was very explicit about the matter. The only question lay in proving the child's affinity to the Negro race, which was not such a difficult matter to do, so the case was quickly settled, since the child's grandmother accompanied him. The judge, however, was irritated. It was a hot day, and he was provoked that such a trivial matter should have taken up his time. He lost his temper as he looked at his watch.

"I don't see why these people want to force their children into the white schools, he declared. There should be a rigid inspection to prevent it, and all the suspected children put out and made to go where they belong."

Pavageau too, was irritated that day. He looked up from some papers which he was folding, and his gaze met Grabért's with a keen, cold, penetrating flash.

"Perhaps Your Honor would like to set the example by taking your son from the schools."

There was an instant silence in the courtroom, a

hush intense and eager. Every eye turned upon the judge, who sat still, a figure carved in stone with livid face and fear-stricken eyes. After the first flash of his eyes, Pavageau had gone on coolly sorting the papers.

The courtroom waited, waited for the judge to rise and thunder forth a fine against the daring Negro lawyer for contempt. A minute passed, which seemed like an hour. Why did not Grabért speak? Pavageau's implied accusation was too absurd for denial; but he should be punished. Was His Honor ill, or did he merely hold the man in too much contempt to notice him or his remark?

Finally Grabért spoke; he moistened his lips, for they were dry and parched, and his voice was weak and sounded far away in his own ears. "My son does not attend the public schools."

Someone in the rear of the room laughed, and the atmosphere lightened at once. Plainly Pavageau was an idiot, and His Honor too far above him; too much of a gentleman to notice him. Grabért continued calmly: "The gentleman—" there was an unmistakable sneer in this word, habit if nothing else, and not even fear could restrain him, "the gentleman doubtless intended a little pleasantry, but I shall have to fine him for contempt of court."

"As you will," replied Pavageau, and he flashed another look at Grabért. It was a look of insolent triumph and derision. His Honor's eyes dropped beneath it.

"What did that man mean, Father, by saying you should take me out of school?" asked Vannier on his way home.

"He was provoked, my son, because he had lost his case, and when a man is provoked, he is likely to say silly things. By the way, Vannier, I hope you won't say anything to your mother about the incident. It would only annoy her."

For the public, the incident was forgotten as soon as it had closed, but for Grabért, it was indelibly stamped on his memory; a scene that shrieked in his mind and stood out before him at every footstep he took. Again and again as he tossed on a sleepless bed did he see the cold flash of Pavageau's eyes, and hear his quiet accusation. How did he know? Where had he gotten his information? For he spoke, not as one who makes a random shot in anger; but as one who knows, who has known a long while, and who is betrayed by irritation into playing his trump card too early in the game.

He passed a wretched week, wherein it seemed that his every footstep was dogged, his every gesture watched and recorded. He fancied that Elise, even, was suspecting him. When he took his judicial seat each morning, it seemed that every eye in the courtroom was fastened upon him in derision; everyone who spoke, it seemed, were but biding their time to shout the old village street refrain which had haunted him all his life, "Nigger! Nigger! White nigger!"

Finally, he could stand it no longer, and with leaden feet and furtive glances to the right and left for fear he might be seen, he went up a flight of dusty stairs in an Exchange Alley building, which led to Pavageau's office.

The latter was frankly surprised to see him. He made a polite attempt to conceal it, however. It was the first time in his legal life that Grabért had ever sought out a Negro; the first time that he had ever voluntarily opened conversation with one.

He mopped his forehead nervously as he took the chair Pavageau offered him; he stared about the room for an instant, then with a sudden, almost brutal directness, he turned on the lawyer.

"See here, what did you mean by that remark you

made in court the other day?"

"I meant just what I said," was the cool reply.

Grabért paused. "Why did you say it?" he asked slowly.

"Because I was a fool. I should have kept my mouth shut until another time, should I not?"

"Pavageau," said Grabért softly, "let's not fence. Where did you get your information?"

Pavageau paused for an instant. He put his fingertips together and closed his eyes as one who meditates. Then he said with provoking calmness, "You seem anxious. Well, I don't mind letting you know. It doesn't really matter."

"Yes, yes," broke in Grabért impatiently.

"Did you ever hear of a Madame Guichard of Hospital Street?"

The sweat broke out on the judge's brow as he replied weakly, "Yes."

"Well, I am her nephew."

"And she?"

"Is dead. She told me about you once. With pride, let me say. No one else knows."

Grabért sat dazed. He had forgotten about Madame Guichard She had never entered into his calculations. Pavageau turned to his desk with a sigh as if he wished the interview were ended. Grabért rose.

"If this were known to my wife," he said thickly, "it would hurt her very much."

His head was swimming. He had had to appeal to this man, and to appeal in his wife's name. His wife, whose name he scarcely spoke to men whom he considered his social equals.

Pavageau looked up quickly. "It happens that I often have cases in your court," he spoke deliberately. "I am willing, if I lose fairly, to give up; but I do not like to have a decision made against me because my opponent is of a different complexion from mine, or because the decision against me would please a certain class of people. I only ask what I have never had from you — fair play."

"I understand," said Grabért.

He admired Pavageau more than ever as he went out of his office, yet this admiration was tempered by the knowledge that this man was the only person in the whole world who possessed positive knowledge of his secret. He groveled in a self-abasement at his position; and yet he could not but feel a certain relief that the vague formless fear which had hitherto dogged his life and haunted it had taken on a definite

shape. He knew where it was now; he could lay his
hands on it and fight it.

But with what weapons? There were none offered
him save a substantial backing down from his
position on certain questions; the position that had
been his for so long that he was almost known by it.
For in the quiet deliberate sentence of Pavageau's, he
read that he must cease all the oppression, all the
little injustices which he had offered Pavageau's
clientele. He must act now as his convictions and
secret sympathies and affiliations had bidden him
act; not as prudence and fear and cowardice had
made him act.

Then what would be the result? he asked himself.
Would not the suspicions of the people be aroused by
this sudden change in his manner? Would they not
begin to question and to wonder? Would not
someone remember Pavageau's remark that morning
and, putting two and two together start some rumor
flying? His heart sickened again at the thought.

There was a banquet that night. It was in his
honor, and he was to speak and the thought was
distasteful to him beyond measure. He knew how it
all would be. He would be hailed with shouts and
acclamations, as the finest flower of civilization. He

would be listened to deferentially, and younger men would go away holding him in their hearts as a truly worthy model. When all the while—

He threw back his head and laughed. Oh, what a glorious revenge he had on those little white village boys! How he had made a race atone for Wilson's insult in the courtroom; for the man in the restaurant at whom Ward had laughed so uproariously; for all the affronts seen and unseen given these people of his own whom he had denied. He had taken a diploma from their most exclusive college; he had broken down the barriers of their social world; he had taken the highest possible position among them; and aping their own ways, had shown them that he too could despise this inferior race they despised. Nay, he had taken for his wife the best woman among them all, and she had borne him a son. Ha, ha! What a joke on them all!

And he had not forgotten the black and yellow boys either. They had stoned him too, and he had lived to spurn them; to look down upon them, and to crush them at every possible turn from his seat on the bench. Truly, his life had not been wasted.

He had lived forty-nine years now, and the zenith of his power was not yet reached. There was much more to do, much more, and he was going to do it. He owed it to Elise and the boy. For their sake he must go on and on and keep his tongue still, and truckle to Pavageau and suffer alone. Someday, perhaps, he would have a grandson, who would point with pride to "my grandfather, the famous Judge Grabért!" Ah, that in itself was a reward. To have founded a dynasty; to bequeath to others that which he had never possessed himself, and the lack of which had made his life a misery.

It was a banquet with a political significance; one that meant a virtual triumph for Judge Grabért in the next contest for the District Judge. He smiled around at the eager faces which were turned up to his as he arose to speak. The tumult of applause which had greeted his rising had died away, and an expectant hush fell on the room.

"What a sensation I could make now," he thought. He had but to open his mouth and cry out, "Fools! Fools! I whom you are honoring, I am one of the despised ones. Yes, I'm a nigger. Do you hear, a nigger!"

What a temptation it was to end the whole miserable farce. If he were alone in the world, if it were not for Elise and the boy, he would, just to see their horror and wonder. How they would shrink from him! But what could they do? They could take away his office; but his wealth, and his former successes, and his learning, they could not touch. Well, he must speak and he must remember Elise and the boy.

Every eye was fixed on him in eager expectancy. Judge Grabért's speech was expected to outline the policy of their faction in the coming campaign. He turned to the chairman at the head of the table.

"Mr. Chairman," he began, and paused again. How peculiar it was that in the place of the chairman there sat Grandmère Grabért as she had been wont to sit on the steps of the tumbledown cottage in the village. She was looking at him sternly and bidding him give an account of his life since she had kissed him goodbye before he had sailed down the river to New Orleans. He was surprised, and not a little annoyed. He had expected to address the chairman, not Grandmère Grabért. He cleared his throat and frowned.

"Mr. Chairman," he said again. Well, what was the use of addressing her that way? She would not understand him. He would call her Grandmère, of course. Were they not alone again on the cottage steps at twilight with the cries of the little brutish boys ringing derisively from the distant village square?

"Grandmère," he said softly, "you don't understand." Then he was sitting down in his seat pointing one finger angrily at her because the other words would not come. They stuck in his throat, and he choked and beat the air with his hands. When the men crowded around him with water and hastily improvised fans, he fought them away wildly and desperately with furious curses that came from his blackened lips. For were they not all boys with stones to pelt him because he wanted to play with them? He would run away to Grandmère, who would soothe him and comfort him. So he arose and, stumbling, shrieking, and beating them back from him, ran the length of the hall and fell across the threshold of the door.

The secret died with him, for Pavageau's lips were ever sealed.

A STORY OF VENGEANCE

Yes, Eleanor, I have grown grayer. I am younger than you, you know, but then, what have you to age you? A kind husband, lovely children, while I am nothing but a lonely woman. Time goes slowly, slowly for me now.

Why did I never marry? Move that screen a little to one side, please; my eyes can scarcely bear a strong light. Bernard? Oh, that's a long story. I'll tell you if you wish; it might pass an hour.

Do you ever think to go over the old schooldays? We thought such foolish things then, didn't we? There wasn't one of us but imagined we would have only to knock ever so faintly on the portals of fame and they would fly wide for our entrance into the magic realms. Or Commencement night we whispered merrily among ourselves on the stage to see our favorite planet, Venus, of course, smiling at us through a high, open window, "bidding adieu to her astronomy class," we said.

Then you went away to plunge into the most brilliant whirl of society, and I stayed in the beautiful old city to work.

Bernard was very much in evidence those days.

He liked you a great deal, because in school-girl parlance you were my 'chum.' You say, thanks, no tea, it reminds me that I'm an old maid. You say you know what happiness means. Maybe, but I don't think any living soul could experience the joy I felt in those days. It was absolutely painful at times.

Byron and his counterparts are ever dear to the womanly heart, whether young or old. Such a man was he, gloomy, misanthropical, tired of the world, with a few dozen broken love affairs among his varied experiences. Of course, I worshipped him secretly, what romantic, silly girl of my age, would not, being thrown in such constant contact with him.

One day he folded me tightly in his arms, and said:

"Little girl, I have nothing to give you in exchange for that priceless love of ours but a heart that has already been at another's feet, and a wrecked life, but may I ask for it?"

"It is already yours," I answered.

I'll draw the veil over the scene which followed; you know, you've 'been there.'

Then began some of the happiest hours that ever the jolly old sun beamed upon, or the love-sick moon clothed in her rays of silver. Deceived me? No, no. He admitted that the old love for Blanche was still in his heart, but that he had lost all faith and respect for her, and could nevermore be other than a friend. Well, I was fool enough to be content with such crumbs.

We had five months of happiness. I tamed down beautifully in that time. Even consented to adopt the peerless Blanche as a model. I gave up all my most ambitious plans and cherished schemes, because he disliked women whose names were constantly in the mouth of the public. In fact, I became quiet, sedate, dignified, renounced too some of my best and dearest friends. I lived, breathed, thought, acted only for him. For me there was but one soul in the universe. Bernard's. Still, for all the suffering I've experienced, I'd be willing to go through it all again just to go over those five months. Every day together, at nights on the lake-shore listening to the soft lap of the waters as the silver sheen of the moon spread over the dainty curled waves, sometimes in a hammock swinging among the trees talking of love and reading poetry. Talk about Heaven! I just think there can't he a better time among the angels.

But there is an end to all things. A violent illness, and his father relenting, sent for the wayward son. I will always believe he loved me, but he was eager to get home to his mother, and anxious to view Blanche in the light of their new relationship. We had a whole series of parting scenes — tears and vows and kisses exchanged. We clung to each other after the regulation fashion, and swore never to forget, and to write every day. Then there was a final wrench. I went back to my old life — he, away home.

For a while I was content, there were daily letters from him to read; his constant admonitions to practice; his many little tokens to adore — until there came a change — letters less frequent, more mention of Blanche and her love for him, less of his love for me, until the truth was forced upon me. Then I grew cold and proud, and with an iron will crushed and stamped all love for him out of my tortured heart and cried for vengeance.

Yes, quite melodramatic, wasn't it? It is a dramatic tale, though.

So I threw off my habits of seclusion and mingled again with men and women, and took up all my long-forgotten plans. It's no use telling you how I succeeded. It was really wonderful, wasn't it? It seems as though that fickle goddess, Fortune, showered every blessing, save one, on my path. Success followed success, triumph succeeded triumph. I was lionized, fêted, petted, caressed by the

social and literary world. You often used to wonder
how I stood it in all those years. God knows; with the
heart-sick weariness and the fierce loathing that
possessed me, I don't know myself.

But, mind you, Eleanor, I schemed well. I had
everything seemingly that humanity craved for, but I
suffered, and by all the gods, I swore that he should
suffer too. Blanche turned against him and married
his brother. An unfortunate chain of circumstances
drove him from his father's home branded as a
forger. Strange, wasn't it? But money is a strong
weapon, and its long arm reaches over leagues and
leagues of land and water.

One day he found me in a distant city, and begged
for my love again, and for mercy and pity. Blanche
was only a mistake, he said, and he loved me alone,
and so on. I remembered all his thrilling tones and
tender glances, but they might have moved granite
now sooner than me. He knelt at my feet and pleaded
like a criminal suing for life. I laughed at him and
sneered at his misery, and told him what he had done
for my happiness, and what I in turn had done for
his.

Eleanor, to my dying day, I shall never forget his
face as he rose from his knees, and with one awful,

indescribable look of hate, anguish and scorn, walked from the room. As he neared the door, all the old love rose in me like a flood, drowning the sorrows of past years, and overwhelming me in a deluge of pity. Strive as I did, I could not repress it. A woman's love is too mighty to be put down with little reasonings. I called to him in terror, "Bernard, Bernard."

He did not turn, gave no sign of having heard.

"Bernard, come back. I didn't mean it."

He passed slowly away with bent head, out of the house and out of my life. I've never seen him since, never heard of him. Somewhere, perhaps on God's earth he wanders outcast, forsaken, loveless. I have my vengeance, but it is like Dead Sea fruit, all bitter ashes to the taste. I am a miserable, heart-weary wreck. A woman with fame, without love.

"Vengeance is an arrow that often falleth and smiteth the hand of him that sent it."

IN OUR NEIGHBORHOOD

The Harts were going to give a party. Neither Mrs. Hart, nor the Misses Hart, nor the small and busy Harts who amused themselves and the neighborhood by continually falling in the gutter on special occasions, had mentioned this fact to anyone, but all the interested denizens of that particular square could tell by the unusual air of bustle and activity which pervaded the Hart domicile. Lillian, who furnished themes for many spirited discussions, leaned airily out of the window, her auburn (red) tresses carefully done in curl papers. Martha, the practical, flourished the broom and duster with unwonted activity, which the small boys of the neighborhood, peering through the green shutters of the front door, duly reported to their mammas, busily engaged in holding down their respective door-steps by patiently sitting thereon.

Pretty soon, the junior Harts — two in number — began to travel to and fro, soliciting the loan of a few chairs, "some nice dishes," and such like things, indispensable to every decent, self-respecting party. But to all inquiries as to the use to which these articles were to be put, they only vouchsafed one reply, "Ma told us as we wasn't to tell, just ask for the things, that's all."

Mrs. Tuckley the dress-maker, brought her sewing out on the front-steps, and entered a vigorous protest to her next door neighbor.

"Humph," she sniffed, "mighty funny they can't say what's up. Must be something in it. Couldn't get none of my things, and not invite me."

"Did she ask you for any?" absentmindedly inquired Mrs. Luke, shielding her eyes from the sun.

"No, but she'd better sense, she knows me. Mercy me, Stella. Just look at that child tumbling in the mud. You, Stella, come here, I say. Look at you now."

The luckless Stella having been soundly cuffed, and sent whimpering in the back-yard, Mrs. Tuckley continued.

"Yes, as I was saying, 'course, taint none o' my business, but I always did wonder how them Harts do keep up. Why, them girls dress just as fine as any lady on the Avenue and that there Lillian wears real diamond ear-rings. 'Pears mighty, mighty funny to me, and Lord the airs they do put on! Holding up their heads like nobody's good enough to speak to. I don't like to talk about people, you know, yourself, Mrs. Luke I never speak about anybody, but mark my word, girls that cut up capers like them Hartses' girls never come to any good."

Mrs. Luke heaved a deep sigh of appreciation at the wisdom of her neighbor, but before she could reply a re-enforcement in the person of little Mrs. Peters, apron over her head, hands shrivelled and soap-sudsy from washing, appeared.

"Did you ever see the like?" she asked in her usual, rapid breathless way. "Louis says they're putting canvass cloths on the floor, and taking down the bed in the back room; and putting greenery and such like trash about. Some style about them, eh?"

Mrs. Tuckley tossed her head and sniffed contemptuously, Mrs. Luke began to rehearse a time worn tale, how once a carriage had driven up to the Hart house at nine o'clock at night, and a distinguished looking man alighted, went in, stayed about ten minutes and finally drove off with a great clatter. Heads that had shaken ominously over this story before began to shake again, and tongues that had wagged themselves tired with conjectures started now with some brand new ideas and theories. The children of the square, tired of fishing for minnows in the ditches, and making mudpies in the street, clustered about their mother's skirts receiving occasional slaps, when their attempts at taking part in the conversation became too pronounced.

Meanwhile, in the Hart household, all was bustle and preparation. To and fro the members of the house flitted, arranging chairs, putting little touches here and there, washing saucers and glasses, chasing the Hart Juniors about, losing things and calling frantically for each other's assistance to find them. Mama Hart, big, plump and perspiring, puffed here and there like a large, rosy engine, giving impossible orders, and receiving sharp answers to foolish questions. Lillian practiced her most graceful poses before the large mirror in the parlor. Martha rushed about, changing the order of the furniture, and Papa Hart, just come in from work, paced the rooms disconsolately, asking for dinner.

"Dinner," screamed Mama Hart, "dinner, who's got time to fool with dinner this evening? Look in the sideboard and you'll see some bread and ham. Eat that and shut up."

Eight o'clock finally arrived, and with it, the music and some straggling guests. When the first faint chee-chee of the violin floated out into the murky atmosphere, the smaller portion of the neighborhood went straightway into ecstasies. Boys and girls in all stages of dishabille clustered about the door-steps and gave vent to audible exclamations of approval or disapprobation concerning the state of affairs behind the green shutters. It was a warm night and the big round moon sailed serenely in a cloudless, blue sky. Mrs. Tuckley had put on a clean calico wrapper, and planted herself with the indomitable Stella on her steps, "to watch the proceedings."

The party was a grand success. Even the intensely critical small fry dancing on the pavement without to the scraping and fiddling of the string band, had to admit that. So far as they were concerned it was all right, but what shall we say of the guests within? They who glided easily over the canvassed floors, bowed, and scraped and simpered, "just like the big folks on the Avenue," who ate the ice-cream and cake, and drank the sweet, weak Catawba wine amid boisterous healths to Mr. and Mrs. Hart and the Misses Hart; who smirked and perspired and cracked ancient jokes and heartrending puns during the intervals of the dances, who shall say that they did not enjoy themselves as thoroughly and as fully as those who frequented the wealthier entertainments up-town.

Lillian and Martha in gossamer gowns of pink and blue flitted to and fro attending to the wants of their guests. Mrs. Hart, gorgeous in a black satin affair, all folds and lace and drapery, made desperate efforts to appear cool and collected, and failed miserably. Papa Hart spent one half his time standing in front of the mantle, spreading out his coattails, and benignly smiling upon the young people, while the other half was devoted to initiating the male portion of the guests into the mysteries of snake killing.

Everybody had said that he or she had had a splendid time, and finally, when the last kisses had been kissed, the last goodbyes been said, the whole Hart family sat down in the now deserted and disordered rooms, and sighed with relief that the great event was over at last.

"Nice crowd, eh?" remarked Papa Hart. He was a brimful of joy and second class whiskey, so no one paid any attention to him.

"But did you see how shamefully Maude flirted with Willie Howard?" said Lillian.

Martha tossed her head in disdain. Mr. Howard she had always considered her especial property, so Lillian's observation had a rather disturbing effect.

"I'm so warm and tired," cried Mama Hart,

plaintively. "Children how are we going to sleep tonight?"

Thereupon the whole family arose to devise ways and means for wooing the drowsy god. As for the Hart Juniors they had long since solved the problem by falling asleep with sticky hands and faces upon a pile of bed-clothing behind the kitchen door.

It was late in the next day before the house had begun to resume anything like its former appearance. The little Harts were kept busy all morning returning chairs and dishes, and distributing the remnants of the feast to the vicinity. The ice-cream had melted into a warm custard, and the cakes had a rather worse for wear appearance, but they were appreciated as much as though just from the confectioner. No one was forgotten, even Mrs. Tuckley, busily stitching on a muslin garment on the steps, and unctuously rolling the latest morsel of scandal under her tongue, was obliged to confess that "them Hartses wasn't such bad people after all, just a bit queer at times."

About two o'clock, just as Lillian was re-draping the tidies on the stiff, common plush chairs in the parlor, someone pulled the bell violently. The visitor, a rather good-looking young fellow with a worried expression smiled somewhat sarcastically as he heard a sound of scuffling and running within the house.

Presently Mrs. Hart opened the door wiping her hand, red and smoking with dish-water, upon her apron. The worried expression deepened on the visitor's face as he addressed the woman with visible embarrassment.

"Er, I-I suppose you are Mrs. Hart?" he inquired awkwardly.

"That's my name, sir," replied she with pretentious dignity.

"Er, may I come in madam?"

"Certainly," and she opened the door to admit him, and offered a chair.

"Your husband is an employee in the Fisher Oil Mills, is he not?"

Mrs. Hart straightened herself with pride as she replied in the affirmative She had always been proud of Mr. Hart's position as foreman of the big oil mills, and was never so happy as when he was expounding to someone in her presence, the difficulties and intricacies of machine work.

"Well, you see my dear Mrs. Hart," continued the visitor. "Now pray don't get excited, there has been an accident, and your husband has, er, been hurt, you know."

But for a painful whitening in her usually rosy face, and a quick compression of her lips, the wife made no sign.

"What was the accident?" she queried, leaning her elbows on her knees.

"Well, you see, I don't understand machinery and the like, but there was something about a wheel out of gear, and a band snapping, or something, anyhow a big wheel flew to pieces, and as he was standing near, he was hit."

"Where?"

"Well, I may as well tell you the truth, madam; a large piece of the wheel struck him on the head and he was killed instantly."

She did not faint, nor make any outcry, nor tear her hair as he had partly expected, but sat still staring at him, with a sort a helpless, dumb horror shining out her eyes, then with a low moan, bowed her head on her knees and shuddered, just as Lillian came in, curious to know what the handsome stranger had to say to her mother.

The poor mutilated body came home at last, and was laid in a stiff, silver-decorated, black coffin in the middle of the sitting-room, which had been made to look as uncomfortable and unnatural as mirrors and furniture shrouded in sheets and mantel and tables divested of ornaments would permit.

There was a wake that night to the unconfined joy of the neighbors, who would rather a burial than a wedding. The friends of the family sat about the coffin, and through the house with long pulled faces. Mrs. Tuckley officiated in the kitchen, making coffee and dispensing cheese and crackers to those who were hungry. As the night wore on, and the first restraint disappeared, jokes were cracked, and quiet laughter indulged in, while the young folks congregated in the kitchen, were hilariously happy, until some member of the family would appear, when every face would sober down.

The older persons contented themselves with recounting the virtues of the deceased, and telling anecdotes wherein he figured largely. It was astonishing how many intimate friends of his had suddenly come to light. Every other man present had either attended school with him, or was a close companion until he died. Proverbs and tales and witty sayings were palmed off as having emanated from his lips. In fact, the dead man would have been surprised himself, had he suddenly come to life and discovered what an important, what a modern solomon he had become.

The long night dragged on, and the people departed in groups of twos and threes, until when the gray dawn crept slowly over the blackness of night shrouding the electric lights in mists of cloudy blue, and sending cold chills of dampness through the house, but a few of the great crowd remained.

The day seemed so gray in contrast to the softening influence of the nigh, the grief which could be hidden then, must now come forth and parade itself before all eyes. There was the funeral to prepare for, the dismal black dresses and bonnets with their long crape veils to don, there were the condolences of sorrowing friends to receive, the floral offerings to be looked at. The little Harts strutted about resplendent in stiff black cravats, and high crape bands about their hats. They were divided between two conflicting emotions — joy at belonging to a family so noteworthy and important, and sorrow at the death. As the time for the funeral approached, and Lillian began to indulge in a series of fainting fits, the latter feeling predominated.

"Well it was all over at last, the family had returned, and as on two nights previous, sat once more in the deserted and dismantled parlor. Mrs. Tuckley and Mrs. Luke, having rendered all assistance possible, had repaired to their respective front steps to keep count of the number of visitors who returned to condole with the family.

"A real nice funeral," remarked the dress-maker at last. "A nice funeral. Everybody took it so hard, and Lillian fainted real beautiful. She's a good girl that Lillian. Poor things, I wonder what they'll do now."

Stella, the irrepressible, was busily engaged balancing herself on one toe, a la ballet.

"Maybe she's going to get married," she volunteered eagerly, " 'cause I saw that yeller-haired young man what comes there all the time, with his arms around her waist, and a telling her not to grieve as he'd take care of her. I was a peeping in the dinin'-room."

"How dare you peep at other folks, and pry into people's affairs? I can't imagine where you get your meddlesome ways from. There ain't none in my family. Next time I catch you at it, I'll spank you good." Then, after a pause, "Well, what else did he say?"

LITTLE MISS SOPHIE

When Miss Sophie knew consciousness again, the long, faint, swelling notes of the organ were dying away in distant echoes through the great arches of the silent church, and she was alone, crouching in a little, forsaken, black heap at the altar of the Virgin. The twinkling tapers seemed to smile pityingly upon her, the beneficent smile of the white-robed Madonna seemed to whisper comfort. A long gust of chill air swept up the aisles, and Miss Sophie shivered, not from cold, but from nervousness.

But darkness was falling, and soon the lights would be lowered, and the great, massive doors would be closed, so gathering her thin little cape about her frail shoulders, Miss Sophie hurried out, and along the brilliant noisy streets home.

It was a wretched, lonely little room, where the cracks let the boisterous wind whistle through, and the smoky, grimy walls looked cheerless and unhomelike. A miserable little room in a miserable little cottage in one of the squalid streets of the Third District that nature and the city fathers seemed to have forgotten.

As bare and comfortless the room, so was Miss

Sophie's lonely life. She rented these four walls from an unkempt little Creole woman, whose progeny seemed like the promised offspring of Abraham — multitudinous. The flickering life in the pale little body she scarcely kept there by the unceasing toil of a pair of bony hands, stitching, stitching, ceaselessly, wearingly on the bands and pockets of pants. It was her bread, this monotonous, unending work, and though while days and nights constant labor brought but the most meagre recompense, it was her only hope of life.

She sat before the little charcoal brazier and warmed her transparent, needlepricked fingers, thinking meanwhile of the strange events of the day. She had been up town to carry the great, black bundle of pants and vests to the factory and receive her small pittance, and on the way home stopped in at the Jesuit Church to say her little prayer at the altar of the calm, white Virgin. There had been a wondrous burst of music from the great organ as she knelt there, an overpowering perfume of many flowers, the glittering dazzle of many lights, and the dainty frou-frou of silken skirts of wedding guests filing and tripping. So Miss Sophie stayed to the wedding, for what feminine heart, be it ever so old and seared, does not delight in one? And why shouldn't a poor little Creole old maid be interested too?

When the wedding party had filed in solemnly, to the rolling, swelling, pealing tones of the organ. Important-looking groomsmen, dainty. fluffy, whiterobed maids, stately, satin-robed, illusion-veiled bride, and happy groom. She leaned forward to catch a better glimpse of their faces. Ah!

Those near the Virgin's altar who heard a faint sigh and rustle on the steps glanced curiously as they saw a slight, black-robed figure clutch the railing and lean her head against it. Miss Sophie had fainted.

"I must have been hungry," she mused over the charcoal fire in her little room, "I must have been hungry," and she smiled a wan smile, and busied herself getting her evening meal of coffee and bread and ham.

If one were given to pity, the first thought that would rush to one's lips at sight of Miss Sophie would have been: Poor little Miss Sophie. She had come among the bareness and sordidness of this neighborhood five years ago, robed in crepe, and crying with great sobs that seemed to fairly shake the vitality out of her. Perfectly silent, too, about her former life, but for all that, Michel, the quarter grocer at the corner, and Mme. Laurent, who kept the shop opposite, had fixed it all up between them, of her sad history and pàst glories. Not that they knew, but then Michel must invent something when the neighbors came to him, their fountain head of wisdom.

One morning little Miss Sophie opened wide her dingy windows to catch the early freshness of the autumn wind as it whistled through the yellow-leafed trees. It was one of those, calm, blue-misted, balmy, November days that New Orleans can have when all the rest of the country is fur-wrapped. Miss Sophie pulled her machine to the window, where the sweet, damp wind could whisk among her black locks.

Whirr, whirr, went the machine, ticking fast and lightly over the belts of the rough jean pants. Whirr, whirr, yes, and Miss Sophie was actually humming a tune. She felt strangely light today.

"Mafoi," muttered Michel, strolling across the street to where Mme. Laurent sat sewing behind the counter on blue and brown-checked aprons, "but the little ma'amselle sings. Perhaps she recollects."

"Perhaps," muttered the rabbe woman.

But little Miss Sophie felt restless. A strange impulse seemed drawing her up town, and the machine seemed to run slow, slow, before it would stitch the endless number of jean belts. Her fingers trembled with nervous haste as she pinned up the unwieldy black bundle of the finished work, and her feet fairly tripped over each other in their eagerness to get to Claiborne Street, where she could board the uptown car. There was a feverish desire to go somewhere, a sense of elation — foolish happiness that brought a faint echo of color into her pinched cheeks. She wondered why.

No one noticed her in the car. Passengers on the Claiborne line are too much accustomed to frail, little blackrobed women with big, black bundles; it is one of the city's most pitiful sights.

She leaned her head out of the window to catch a glimpse of the oleanders on Bayou Road, when her attention was caught by a conversation in the car.

"Yes, it's too bad for Neale, and lately married too," said the elder man, "I can't see what he is to do."

She pricked up her ears. Neale. That was the name of the groom in the Jesuit church.

"How did it happen?" languidly inquired the younger. He was a stranger, evidently, a stranger with a high regard for the faultlessness of male attire, too.

"Well, the firm failed first; he didn't mind that much, he was so sure of his uncle's inheritance repairing his lost fortunes, but suddenly this difficulty of identification springs up, and he is literally on the verge of ruin."

"Won't some of you fellows who've known him all your lives do to identify him?"

"Gracious man, we've tried, but the absurd old will expressly stipulates that he shall be known only by a certain quaint Roman ring, and unless he has it — no identification, no fortune. He has given the ring away and that settles it."

"Well, you're all chumps. Why doesn't he get the ring from the owner?"

"Easily said. It seems that Neale had some little Creole love-affair some years ago and gave this ring to his dusky-eyed fiancée. But you know how Neale is with his love-affairs, went off and forgot the girl in a month. It seems, however, she took it to heart. So much so until he's ashamed to try to find her or the ring."

Miss Sophie heard no more as she gazed out into the dusty grass. There were tears in her eyes, hot blinding ones that wouldn't drop for pride, but stayed and scalded. She knew the story with all its embellishments of heartaches. The ring too. She remembered the day she had kissed and wept and fondled it, until it seemed her heart must burst under its load of grief before she took it to the pawn broker's that another might be eased before the end came — that other, her father. The "little Creole love affair" of Neale's had not always been poor and old and jaded-looking. But reverses must come, even Neale knew that. So the ring was at the Mont de Piété.

Still he must have it, it was his. It would save him from disgrace and suffering, and from trailing the proud head of the white-gowned bride into sorrow. He must have it. But how?

There it was still at the pawn-broker's, no one would have such a jewel, and the ticket was home in the bureau drawer. Well, he must have it. She might starve in the attempt. Such a thing as going to him and telling him that he might redeem it was an impossibility. That good, straight-backed, stiff-necked Creole blood would have risen in all its strength and choked her. No, as a present had the quaint Roman circlet been placed upon her finger. As a present should it be returned.

The bumping car rode heavily, and the hot

thoughts beat heavily in her poor little head. He must have the ring, but how. The ring. The Roman ring. The white-robed bride starving. She was going mad. Ah yes, the church.

Right in the busiest, most bustling part of the town, its fresco and bronze and iron quaintly suggestive of medieval times. Within, all cool and dim and restful, with the faintest whiff of lingering incense rising and pervading the gray arches. Yes, the Virgin would know and have pity. The sweet, whiterobed Virgin at the pretty flower-decked altar, or the one away up in the niche, far above the golden dome where the Host was. Holy Mary, Mother of God. Poor little Miss Sophie.

Titiche, the busy-body of the house, noticed that Miss Sophie's bundle was larger than usual that afternoon. "Ah, poor woman," sighed Titiche's mother, "she would be rich for Christmas."

The bundle grew larger each day, and well worth her toil, she thought, to have it again.

Had Titiche not been shooting crackers on the banquette instead of peering into the crack, as was his wont, his big, round, black eyes would have grown saucer-wide to see little Miss Sophie kiss and fondle a ring, an ugly clumsy band of gold.

"Ah, dear ring," she murmured, "once you were his, and you shall be his again. You shall be on his finger, and perhaps touch his heart. Dear ring, *ma chere petite, de ma coeur, cheri, de ma coeur. Je t'aime, je t'aime, oui, ozzi.* You are his, you were mine once too. Tonight just one night, I'll keep you. Then tomorrow, you can save him.

"Ah, the Virgin. She smiles at me because I did right, did I not sweet mother? She smiles and I grow faint—"

The loud whistles and horns of the little ones rose on t he balmy air next morning. No one would doubt it was Christmas Day, even if doors and windows are open wide to let in cool air. Why, there was Christmas even in the very look of the mules on the poky cars. There was Christmas noise in the streets, and Christmas toys and Christmas odors, savory ones that made the nose wrinkle approvingly, issuing from the kitchen. Michel and Mme. Laurent smiled greetings across the street at each other and the salutation from a passer-by recalled the many progenied landlady to herself.

"Miss Sophie, well, poor soul, not very much Christmas for her. *Mais,* I'll just call her in to spend the day with me. It'll cheer her a bit."

So clean and orderly within the poor little room not a speck of dust or a litter of any kind on the quaint little old time high bureau, unless you might except a sheet of paper lying loose with something written on it. Titiche had evidently inherited his prying propensities for the landlady turned it over and read:

Louis.
Here is the ring. I return it to you. I heard you needed it, I hope it comes not too late.
Sophie.

"The ring, where?" muttered the landlady.

There it was, clasped between her fingers on her bosom. A bosom, white and cold, under a cold, happy face. Christmas had indeed dawned for Miss Sophie — the eternal Christmas.

AT EVENTIDE

All day had she watched and waited for his coming, and still her strained ears caught no sounds of the footsteps she loved and longed to hear. All day while the great sun panted on his way around the brazen skies. All day while the busy world throbbed its mighty engines of labor, breaking hearts in its midst. And now when the eve had come, and the sun sank slowly to rest, casting his red rays over the earth he loved, and bidding tired nature a gentle radiant goodnight, she still watched and waited. Waited while the young moon shone silvery in the crimson flush of the eastern sky, while the one bright star trembled as he strove to near his love; waited while the hum of soul-wearing traffic died in the distant streets, and the merry voices of happy children floated to her ears.

And still he came not. What kept him from her side? Had he learned the cold lesson of self-control, or found one other thing more potent than love? Had some cruel chain of circumstances forced him to disobey her bidding, or did he love another? But no, she smiles triumphantly, he could not having known and loved her.

Sitting in the deep imbrasure of the window through which the distant wave sounds of city life floated to her, the pages of her life seemed to turn back, and she read the almost forgotten tale of long ago, the story of their love. In those days his wish had been her law, his smile her sun, his frown her wretchedness. Within his arms, earth seemed a far-away dream of empty nothingness, and when his lips touched and clung to hers, sweet with the perfume of the South they floated away into a Paradise of space, where Time and Death and the woes of this great earth are naught, only these two — and love, the almighty.

And so their happiness drifted slowly across the sea of Time until it struck a cruel rock, whose sharp teeth showed not above the dimpled waves. Where once had been a craft of strength and beauty, now was only a hideous wreck. For the Tempter had come into this Eden, and soon his foul whisper found place in her heart.

And the Tempter's name was Ambition.

Often had the praises and plaudits of men rang in her ears when her sweet voice sang to her chosen friends, often had the tears evoked by her songs of love and hope and trust. thrilled her breast faintly, as the young bird sits in its nest under the loving mother's wing, but he had clasped his arms around her, and that was enough. But one day the Tempter whispered, "Why waste such talent? Bring that beauty of voice before the world and see men bow in homage, and women envy and praise. Come forth and follow me."

But she put him fiercely aside. and cried, "I want no homage but his, I want no envy from anyone."

Still the whisper stayed in her heart, nor would the honeyed words of praise be gone, even when he kissed her, and thanked the gods for this pearl of great price.

Then as time fled on, the tiny whisper grew into a great roar, and all the praise of men, and the sweet words of women, filled her brain, and what had once been her aversion became a great desire, and caused her brow to grow thoughtful, and her eyes moody.

But when she spoke to him of this new love, he smiled and said, "My wife must be mine, and mine alone. I want not a woman whom the world claims, and shouts her name abroad. My wife and my home must by inviolate."

And again as of yore, his wish controlled her. But only for a while.

Then the tiny whisper grown into the great roar urging her on, became a mighty wind which drove her before it, nor could she turn aside from the path of ambition, but swept on, and conquered.

Ah, sweet, sweet the exultation of the victor. Dear the plaudits of the admiring world. Wild the joy, when queen of song, admired of men, she stood upon the pinnacle of fame. And he? True to his old convictions, turned sadly from the woman who placed the admiration of the world before his love and the happiness of his home, and went out from her life broken-hearted, disappointed, miserable.

All these things, and more, she thought upon in the first flush of eventide, as the bold, young star climbed toward his lady-love, the moon, all these things, and what had come to pass after the victory.

For there came a day when the world wearied of its toy, and turned with shouts of joy, and wreaths of fresh laurels for the new star. Then came disappointments and miseries crowding fast upon her. The sorrows which a loving heart knows when its finds its idols faithless. Then the love for him which she had once repressed arose in all its strength which had gained during the long struggle with the world, arose and overwhelmed her with its might, and filled her soul with an unutterable longing for peace and rest and him.

She wrote to him and told him all her heart, and begged of him to come back to her, for Fame was but an empty bubble while love was supreme and the only happiness, after all. And now she waited while the crimson and gold of the west grew dark, and gray and lowering.

Hark! She hears his loved step. He comes, ah, joy of heaven he comes. Soon will he clasp her in his arms, and there on his bosom shall she know peace and rest and love.

As he enters the door she hastens to meet him, the love-light shining in her tired eyes, her soft rounded arms outstretched to meet him. But he folds her not in his embrace, nor yet does he look with love into her upturned eyes. The voice she loves, ah so well, breaks upon the dusky silence, pitiless, stern.

"Most faithless of faithless women, think you that like the toy of a fickle child I can be thrown aside, then picked up again? Think you that I can take a soiled lily to my bosom? Think you that I can cherish the gaudy sun-flower that ever turns to the broad, brazen glare of the uncaring sun, rather than the modest shrinking, violet? Nay, be not deceived, I loved you once, but that love you killed in its youth and beauty leaving me to stand and weep alone over its grave. I came tonight, not to kiss you, and to forgive you as you entreat, but to tell that you I have wed another."

The pitiless voice ceased, and she was alone in the dusky silence. Alone in all the shame and agony and grief of unrequited love and worthless fame. Alone to writhe and groan in despair while the roseate flush of eventide passed into the coldness of midnight.

Oh faithless woman, oh, faithless man. How frail the memory of thy binding vows, thy blissful hours of love. Are they forgotten? Only the record of broken hearts and loveless lives will show.

THE BEE MAN

We were glancing over the mental photograph album, and commenting on the great lack of dissimilarity in tastes. Nearly everyone preferred spring to any other season, with a very few exceptions in favor of autumn. The women loved Mrs. Browning and Longfellow. The men showed decided preferences after Emerson and Macauley. Conceit stuck out when the majority wanted to be themselves and none other. Only two did not want to live in the present century. But in one place, in answer to the question, "Whom would you rather be, if not yourself?" the answer was, "A baby."

"Why would you rather be a baby than any other personage?" queried someone glancing at the writer, who blushed as she replied.

"Because then I might be able to live a better life, I might have better opportunities and better chances for improving them, and it would bring me nearer the 20th century."

"About eight or nine years ago," said the first speaker, "I remember reading a story in a magazine for young folks. It was merely a fairy story, and perhaps was not intended to point a moral, but only to amuse the little ones. It was something on this order:

Once upon a time, there lived in an out of the way spot an ancient decrepit bee man. How old he was no one knew. Whence he came, no one could tell: to the memory of the oldest inhabitant he had always lived in his dirty hut, surrounded by myriads of hives, attended always by a swarm of bees. He was good to the bits of children, and always ready with a sweet morsel of honeycomb for them. All his ambitions, sympathies and hopes were centered in his hives. Until one day a fairy crept into his hut and whispered:

"You have not always been a common bee man. Once you were something else."

"Tell me what I was," he asked eagerly.

"Nay, that I cannot do," replied the fairy, "our queen sent me to tell you this, and if you wished to search for your former self, I am to assist you. You must search the entire valley, and the first thing you meet to which you become violently attached, that is what you formerly were and I shall give you back your correct form."

So the next morning the Bee Man, strapping his usual hive upon his back, and accompanied by the fairy in the form of a queen bee, set out upon his search throughout the valley. At first he became violently attached to the handsome per-on and fine castle of the Lord of the Realm, but on being kicked out of the lord's domains, his love turned to dislike.

The Bee Man and the fairy travelled far and wide and carefully inspected every thing they met. The very Imp, the Languid young man, the Hippogriffith, the Thousand Tailed Hippotamus, and many other types, until the Bee Man grew weary and was about to give up t e search in disgust.

But suddenly amid all the vast halls of the enchanted domains through which they were wandering, there sounded shrieks and wails, and the inmates were thrown into the greatest confusion by the sight of the hideous hippogriffith dashing through, a million sparks emanating from his great eyes, his barbed tail waving high in the air, and holding in his talons a tiny infant.

Now, as soon as the Bee Man saw this, a great wave of sorrow and pity filled his breast,,and he hastily followed the monster, arriving at his cave just in time to see him preparing to devour his prey. Madly dashing his hive of bees in o the hippogriffith's face, and seizing the infant while the disturbed and angry bees stung and swarmed, the Bee Man rushed out followed by the very Imp, the Languid young man and the fairy. and made his way to the child's mother. Just as soon as the baby was safely restored, the Bee Man ruminated thoughtfully a while and finally remarked to the fairy:

"Do you know of all the things I have met so far. I liked the baby best of all, so I think I must have been a baby once."

"Right you are," assented the fairy. "I knew it before, but of course, I couldn't tell. Now I shall change you into your former shape. But remember, you must try to be something better than a bee man."

The Bee Man promised and was instantly changed into a baby. The fairy inoculated him from harm with a bee sting, and gave him to the rescued infant's mother.

Nearly a cycle passed by. One day the fairy, having business in the valley, thought she would make inquiries concerning her protégé. In her way she happened to pass a little, low, curious hut, with many beehives about it, and swarms of bees flying in and out. The fairy, tired as well as curious, peeped in and discovered an ancient man attending to the wants of his pets. Upon a closer inspection. she recognized her infant of years ago. He had become a bee man again."

"It points to a pretty little moral," said the Fatalist, "for it proves that do what we will, we cannot get away from our natures. It was inherent in that man's nature to tend bees. Bee-ing was the occupation chosen for him by Fate, and had the beneficent Fairy changed him a dozen times, he would ultimately have gone to bee-ing in some form or other."

The Fatalist was doubtless right. It seems as though the inherent things in our nature must come out. The ancient bee man, perhaps is but a type of humanity growing old, and settled in its mode of living, while the fairy is but thought, whispering into our souls things half dread half pleasant.

There are moments when the consciousness of a former life comes sharply upon us, in swift, lightning flashes, too sudden to be tangible, too dazzling to leave an impress, or perhaps, in troubled dreams that bewilder and confuse with vague remembrances. If only a burst of memory would come upon some mortal, that the tale might be fully told, and these theories established as facts. It would unfold great possibilities of historical lore, of literary life, of religious speculation.

THE GOODNESS OF SAINT ROCQUE

MANUELA was tall and slender and graceful, and once you knew her the lithe form could never be mistaken. She walked with the easy spring that comes from a perfectly arched foot. today she swept swiftly down Marais Street, casting a quick glance here and there from under her heavy veil as if she feared she was being followed. If you had peered under the veil, you would have seen that Manuela's dark eyes were swollen and discoloured about the lids, as though they had known a sleepless, tearful night.

There had been a picnic the day before, and as merry a crowd of giddy, chattering Creole girls and boys as ever you could see boarded the ramshackle dummy-train that puffed its way wheezily out wide Elysian Fields Street, around the lily-covered bayous, to Milneburg-on-the-Lake. Now, a picnic at Milneburg is a thing to be remembered for ever. One charters a rickety-looking, weather-beaten dancing-pavilion, built over the water, and after storing the children — for your true Creole never leaves the small folks at home — and the baskets and mothers downstairs, the young folks go upstairs and dance to the tune of the best band you ever heard. For what can equal the music of a violin, a guitar, a cornet, and a bass viol to trip the quadrille to at a picnic?

Then one can fish in the lake and go bathing under the prim bath-houses, so severely separated sexually, and go rowing on the lake in a trim boat, followed by the shrill warnings of anxious mothers. And in the evening one comes home, hat crowned with cool gray Spanish moss, hands burdened with fantastic latanier baskets woven by the brown bayou boys, hand in hand with your dearest one, tired but happy.

At this particular picnic, however, there had been bitterness of spirit. Theophile was Manuela's own especial property, and Theophile had proven false. He had not danced a single waltz or quadrille with Manuela, but had deserted her for Claralie, blonde and petite. It was Claralie whom Theophile had rowed out on the lake. It was Claralie whom Theophile had gallantly led to dinner. It was Claralie's hat that he wreathed with Spanish moss, and Claralie whom he escorted home after the jolly singing ride in town on the little dummy-train.

Not that Manuela lacked partners or admirers. Dear no, she was too graceful and beautiful for that. There had been more than enough for her. But

Manuela loved Theophile, you see, and no one could take his place. Still, she had tossed her head and let her silvery laughter ring out in the dance, as though she were the happiest of mortals, and had tripped home with Henri, leaning on his arm, and looking up into his eyes as though she adored him.

This morning she showed the traces of a sleepless night and an aching heart as she walked down Marais Street. Across wide St. Rocque Avenue she hastened. "Two blocks to the river and one below," she repeated to herself breathlessly. Then she stood on the corner gazing about her, until with a final summoning of a desperate courage she dived through a small wicket gate into a garden of weed-choked flowers.

There was a hoarse, rusty little bell on the gate that gave querulous tongue as she pushed it open. The house that sat back in the yard was little and old and weather-beaten. Its one-story frame had once been painted, but that was a memory remote and traditional. A straggling morning-glory strove to conceal its time-ravaged face. The little walk of broken bits of brick was reddened carefully, and the one little step was scrupulously yellow-washed, which denoted that the occupants were cleanly as well as religious.

Manuela's timid knock was answered by a harsh *"Entrez."*

It was a small sombre room within, with a bare yellow-washed floor and ragged curtains at the little window. In a corner was a diminutive altar draped with threadbare lace. The red glow of the taper lighted a cheap print of St. Joseph and a brazen crucifix. The human element in the room was furnished by a little, wizened yellow woman, who, black-robed, turbaned, and stern, sat before an uncertain table whereon were greasy cards.

Manuela paused, her eyes blinking at the semi-obscurity within. The Wizened One called in croaking tones:

"And for why you come here? *Assiez-la*, ma'amzelle."

Timidly Manuela sat at the table facing the owner of the voice.

"I want," she began faintly, but the Mistress of the Cards understood, she had had much experience. The cards were shuffled in her long grimy talons and stacked before Manuela.

"Now you cut dem in three part, so — *un, deux, trois, bien*. You make your wish with all your heart, *bien.* Yes, I see, I see."

Breathlessly did Manuela learn that her lover was true, but "that light gal, yes, she mek' nouvena in St. Rocque for his love."

"I give you one lil' charm, yes," said the Wizened One when the seance was over, and Manuela, all white and nervous, leaned back in the rickety chair. "I give you one lil' charm for to ween him back, yes. You wear it around your waist, an' he come back. Then you make prayer at St. Rocque and burn candle. Then you come back and tell me, yes. *Cinquante sous, ma'amzelle. Merci.* Good luck go with you."

Readjusting her veil, Manuela passed out the little wicket gate, treading on air. Again the sun shone, and the breath of the swamps came as healthful sea-breeze unto her nostrils. She fairly flew in the direction of St. Rocque.

There were quite a number of persons entering the white gates of the cemetery. This was Friday, when all who wish good luck pray to the saint and wash their steps promptly at twelve o'clock with a wondrous mixture to guard the house. Manuela bought a candle from the keeper of the little lodge at the entrance, and pausing one instant by the great sun-dial to see if the heavens and the hour were propitious, glided into the tiny chapel, dim and stifling with heavy air from myriad wish-candles blazing on the wide table before the altar-rail. She said her prayer and lighting her candle placed it with the others.

How brightly the sun seemed to shine now, she thought, pausing at the door on her way out. Her small fingertips, still bedewed with holy water, rested caressingly on a gamin's head. The ivy which enfolds the quaint chapel never seemed so green, the shrines which serve as the Way of the Cross never seemed so artistic, the baby graves, even, seemed cheerful.

Theophile called Sunday. Manuela's heart leaped. He had been spending his Sundays with Claralie. His stay was short and he was plainly bored. But Manuela knelt to thank the good St. Rocque that night, and fondled the charm about her slim waist. There came a box of bonbons during the week, with a decorative card all roses and fringe, from Theophile. But being a Creole, and therefore superstitiously careful, and having been reared by a wise and experienced mother to mistrust the gifts of a recreant lover, Manuela quietly thrust bonbons, box, and card into the kitchen fire, and the Friday following placed the second candle of her nouvena in St. Rocque.

Manuela's friends had watched with indignation

Theophile gallantly leading Claralie home from High Mass on Sunday. They gasped with astonishment when, the next Sunday, with his usual bow, the young man offered Manuela his arm as the worshippers filed out in step to the organ's march. Claralie tossed her head as she crossed herself with holy water. The pink in her cheeks was brighter than usual.

Manuela smiled a bright good morning when she met Claralie in St. Rocque the next Friday. The little blonde blushed furiously, and Manuela rushed post-haste to the Wizened One to confer upon this new issue.

"It is good," said the dame, shaking her turbaned head. "She is afraid, she will work, *mais* your charm, it will beat her."

And Manuela departed with radiant eyes.

Theophile was not at Mass Sunday morning, and murderous glances flashed from Claralie to Manuela before the tinkling of the Host-Bell. Nor did Theophile call at either house. Two hearts beat furiously at the sound of every passing footstep,,and two minds wondered if the other were enjoying the beloved one's smiles. Two pair of eyes, however, blue and black, smiled on others, and their owners laughed and seemed none the less happy. For your Creole girls are proud, and would die rather than let the world see their sorrows.

Monday evening Theophile, the missing, showed his rather sheepish countenance in Manuela's parlour, and explained that he, with some chosen spirits, had gone for a trip "over the lake."

"I did not ask you where you were yesterday," replied the girl, saucily.

Theophile shrugged his shoulders and changed the conversation.

The next week there was a birthday fête in honour of Louise, Theophile's young sister. Everyone was bidden, and no one thought of refusing, for Louise was young, and this would be her first party. So, though the night was hot, the dancing went on as merrily as light young feet could make it go. Claralie fluffed her dainty white skirts, and cast mischievous sparkles in the direction of Theophile, who with the mother and Louise was bravely trying not to look self-conscious. Manuela, tall and calm and proud-looking, in a cool, pale yellow gown was apparently enjoying herself without paying the slightest attention to her young host.

"Have I the pleasure of this dance?" he asked her finally, in a lull of the music.

She bowed assent, and as if moved by a common

impulse they strolled out of the dancing-room into the cool, quaint garden, where jessamines gave out an overpowering perfume, and a caged mocking-bird complained melodiously to the full moon in the sky.

It must have been an engrossing conversation, for the call to supper had sounded twice before they heard and hurried in with Louise radiantly leading on the arm of papa, Claralie with Leon and Theophile and Manuela bringing up the rear.

In the dining room, Theophile proudly led his partner to the head of the table, at the right hand of mother. When a Creole man places a girl at his mother's right hand at his own table, there is but one conclusion to be deduced therefrom.

If you had asked Manuela, after the wedding was over, how it happened, she would have said nothing, but looked wise. If you had asked Claralie, she would have laughed and said she always preferred Leon. If you had asked Theophile, he would have wondered that you thought he had ever meant more than to tease Manuela. If you had asked the Wizened One, she would have offered you a charm.

St. Rocque knows, for he is a good saint, and if you believe in him and are true and good, and make your nouvenas with a clean heart, he will grant your wish.

THE FISHERMAN OF PASS CHRISTIAN

THE swift breezes on the beach at Pass Christian meet and conflict as though each strove for the mastery of the air. The land-breeze blows down through the pines, resinous, fragrant, cold, bringing breath-like memories of dim, dark woods shaded by myriad pine needles. The breeze from the Gulf is warm and soft and languorous, blowing up from the south with its suggestion of tropical warmth and passion. It is strong and masterful, and tossed Annette's hair and whipped her skirts about her in bold disregard for the proprieties.

Arm in arm with Philip, she was strolling slowly down the great pier which extends from the Mexican Gulf Hotel into the waters of the Sound. There was no moon tonight, but the sky glittered and scintillated with myriad stars, brighter than you can ever see farther North, and the great waves that the Gulf breeze tossed up in restless profusion gleamed with the white fire of phosphorescent flame. The wet sands on the beach glowed white fire, the posts of the pier where the waves had leapt and left a laughing kiss, the sides of the little boats and fish-cars tugging at their ropes, alike showed white and flaming, as though the sea and all it touched were afire.

Annette and Philip paused midway the pier to watch two fishermen casting their nets. With heads bared to the breeze, they stood in clear silhouette against the white background of sea.

"See how he uses his teeth," almost whispered Annette.

Drawing himself up to his full height, with one end of the huge seine between his teeth, and the cord in his left hand, the taller fisherman of the two paused a half instant, his right arm extended, grasping the folds of the net. There was a swishing rush through the air, and it settled with a sort of sob as it cut the waters and struck a million sparkles of fire from the waves. Then, with backs bending under the strain, the two men swung on the cord, drawing in the net, laden with glittering restless fish, which were unceremoniously dumped on the boards to be put into the fish-car awaiting them.

Philip laughingly picked up a soft, gleaming jelly-fish, and threatened to put it on Annette's neck. She screamed, ran, slipped on the wet boards, and in another instant would have fallen over into the water below. The tall fisherman caught her in his arms and set her on her feet.

"Mademoiselle must be very careful," he said in the softest and most correct French. "The tide is in and the water very rough. It would be very difficult to swim out there tonight."

Annette murmured confused thanks, which were supplemented by Philip's hearty tones. She was silent until they reached the pavilion at the end of the pier. The semi-darkness was unrelieved by lantern or light. The strong wind wafted the strains from a couple of mandolins, a guitar, and a tenor voice stationed in one corner to sundry engrossed couples in sundry other corners. Philip found an untenanted nook and they ensconced themselves therein.

"Do you know there's something mysterious about that fisherman?" said Annette, during a lull in the wind.

"Because he did not let you go over?" inquired Philip.

"No, he spoke correctly, and with the accent that goes only with an excellent education."

Philip shrugged his shoulders.

"That's nothing remarkable. If you stay about Pass Christian for any length of time, you'll find more things than perfect French and courtly grace among fishermen to surprise you. These are a wonderful people who live across the Lake."

Annette was lolling in the hammock

under the big catalpa-tree some days later, when the gate opened, and Natalie's big sun-bonnet appeared. Natalie herself was discovered blushing in its dainty depths. She was only a little Creole seaside girl, you must know, and very shy of the city demoiselles. Natalie's patois was quite as different from Annette's French as it was from the postmaster's English.

"Miss Annette," she began, surprised at her own boldness, "we will have one lil' hay-ride this night, and a fish-fry at the end. Will you come?"

Annette sprang to her feet in delight. "Will I come? Certainly. How delightful. You are so good to ask me."

But Natalie's pink bonnet had fled precipitately down the shaded walk. Annette laughed joyously as Philip lounged down the gallery.

"I frightened the child away," she told him.

You've never been for a hay-ride and fish-fry on the shores of the Mississippi Sound, have you? When the summer boarders and the Northern visitors undertake to give one, it is a comparatively staid affair, where due regard is had for one's wearing apparel, and where there are servants to do the hardest work. Then it isn't enjoyable at all. But when the natives, the boys and girls who live there, make up their minds to have fun, you may depend upon its being just the best kind.

This time there were twenty boys and girls, a mamma or so, several papas, and a grizzled fisherman to restrain the ardor of the amateurs. The cart was t vast and solid, and two comfortable, sleepy-looking mules constituted the drawing power. There were also tin horns, some guitars, an accordion and a quartet of much praised voices. The hay in the bottom of the wagon was freely mixed with pine needles, whose prickiness through your hose was amply compensated for by its delicious fragrance.

After a triumphantly noisy passage down the beach one comes to the stretch of heavy sand that lies between Pass Christian proper and Henderson's Point. This is a hard pull for the mules, and the more ambitious riders get out and walk. Then, after a final strain through the shifting sands, bravo, the shell road is reached, and one goes cheering through the pine-trees to Henderson's Point.

If ever you go to Pass Christian, you must have a fish-fry at Henderson's Point. It is the pine-thicketed,

whitebeached peninsula jutting out from the land,
with one side caressed by the waters of the Sound
and the other purred over by the blue waves of the
Bay of St. Louis. Here is the beginning of the great
three-mile trestle bridge to the town of Bay St. Louis,
and tonight from the beach could be seen the lights of
the villas glittering across the Bay like myriads of
unsleeping eyes.

Here upon a firm stretch of white sand camped the
merry-makers. Soon a great fire of driftwood and
pine cones tossed its flames defiantly at a radiant
moon in the sky, and the fishers were casting their
nets in the sea. The more daring of the girls waded
barelegged in the water, holding pinetorches,
spearing flounders and peering for soft-shell crabs.

Annette had wandered farther in the shallow
water than the rest. Suddenly she stumbled against a
stone, the torch dropped and spluttered at her feet.
With a little helpless cry she looked at the stretch of
unfamiliar beach and water to find herself all alone.

"Pardon me, mademoiselle," said a voice at her
elbow, "you are in distress?"

It was her fisherman, and with a scarce conscious
sigh of relief, Annette put her hand into the
outstretched one at her side.

"I was looking for soft shells," she explained, "and lost the crowd, and now my torch is out."

"Where is the crowd?"

There was some amusement in the tone, and Annette glanced up quickly, prepared to be thoroughly indignant at this fisherman who dared make fun at her, but there was such a kindly look about his mouth that she was reassured and said meekly:

"At Henderson's Point."

"You have wandered a half mile away," he mused, "and have nothing to show for your pains but very wet skirts. If mademoiselle will permit me, I will take her to her friends, but allow me to suggest that mademoiselle will leave the water and walk on the sands."

"But I am barefoot," wailed Annette, "and I am afraid of the fiddlers."

Fiddler crabs, you know, aren't pleasant things to be dangling around one's bare feet, and they are more numerous than sand fleas down at Henderson's Point.

"True," assented the fisherman, "then we shall have to wade back."

The fishing was over when they rounded the point

and- came in sight of the cheery bonfire with its Rembrandt-like group, and the air was savoury with the smell of frying fish and crabs. The fisherman was not to be tempted by appeals to stay, but smilingly disappeared down the sands, the red glare of his torch making a glowing track in the water.

"Ah, Miss Annette," whispered Natalie, between mouthfuls of a rich croaker, "you have found a beau in the water."

"And the fisherman of the Pass, too," laughed her cousin Ida.

Annette tossed her head, for Philip had growled audibly.

"Do you know, Philip," cried Annette a few days after, rudely shaking him from his siesta on the gallery, "do you know that I have found my fisherman's hut?"

"Hum," was the only response.

"Yes, and it's the quaintest, most delightful spot imaginable. Philip, do come with me and see it."

"Hum."

"Oh, Philip, you are so lazy, do come with me."

"Yes, but, my dear Annette," protested Philip, "this is a warm day, and I am tired."

Still, his curiosity being aroused, he went

grumbling. It was not a very long drive, back from the beach across the railroad and through the pine forest to the bank of a dark, slow-flowing bayou. The fisherman's hut was small, two-roomed, whitewashed, pineboarded, with the traditional mud chimney acting as a sort of support to one of its uneven sides. Within was a weird assortment of curios from every uncivilized part of the globe. Also were there fishing-tackle and guns in reckless profusion. The fisherman, in the kitchen of the mud-chimney, was sardonically waging war with a basket of little bayou crabs.

"Entrez, mademoiselle et monsieur," he said pleasantly, grabbing a vicious crab by its flippers, and smiling at its wild attempts to bite. "You see I am busy, but make yourself at home."

"Well, how on earth—" began Philip.

"Sh!" whispered Annette. "I was driving out in the woods this morning, and stumbled on the hut. He asked me in, but I came right over after you."

The fisherman, having succeeded in getting the last crab in the kettle of boiling water, came forward smiling and began to explain the curios.

"Then you have not always lived at Pass

Christian," said Philip.

"Mais non, monsieur, I am spending a summer here."

"And he spends his winters, doubtless, selling fish in the French market," spitefully soliloquised Philip.

The fisherman was looking unutterable things into Annette's eyes, and, it seemed to Philip, taking an unconscionably long time explaining the use of an East Indian stiletto.

"Oh, wouldn't it be delightful," came from Annette at last.

"What?" asked Philip.

"Why, Monsieur LeConte says he'll take six of us out in his catboat tomorrow for a fishing-trip on the Gulf."

"Hum," drily.

"And I'll get Natalie and her cousins."

"Yes," still more drily.

Annette chattered on, entirely oblivious of the strainedness of the men's adieux, and still chattered as they drove through the pines.

"I did not know that you were going to take fishermen and merchants into the bosom of your social set when you came here," growled Philip, at last.

"But, Cousin Phil, can't you see he is a gentleman? The fact that he makes no excuses or protestations is a proof."

"You are a fool," was the polite response.

Still, at six o'clock next morning, there was a little crowd of seven upon the pier, laughing and chatting at the little 'Virginie' dipping her bows in the water and flapping her sails in the brisk wind. Natalie's pink bonnet blushed in the early sunshine, and Natalie's mamma, comely and portly, did chaperonage duty. It was not long before the sails gave swell into the breeze and the little boat scurried to the Sound. Past the lighthouse on its gawky iron stalls, she flew, and now rounded the white sands of Cat Island.

"Bravo, the Gulf," sang a voice on the lookout. The little boat dipped, halted an instant, then sailed fast into the blue Gulf waters.

"We will anchor here," said the host, "have luncheon, and fish."

Philip couLd not exactly understand why the fisherman should sit so close to Annette and whisper so much into her ears. He chafed at her acting the part of hostess, and was possessed of a murderous desire to throw the pink sun-bonnet and its owner into the sea, when Natalie whispered audibly to one of her cousins that "Miss Annette act nice wit' her lover."

The sun was banking up flaming pillars of rose and gold in the west when the little 'Virginie' rounded Cat Island on her way home, and the quick Southern twilight was fast dying into darkness when she was tied up to the pier and the merry-makers sprang off with baskets of fish. Annette had distinguished herself by catching one small shark, and had immediately ceased to fish and devoted her attention to her fisherman and his line. Philip had angled fiercely, landing trout, croakers, sheep's head, snappers in bewildering luck. He had broken each hopeless captive's neck savagely, as though they were personal enemies. He did not look happy as they landed, though lots of praise were being sung in his honour.

As the days passed on, the fisherman of the Pass began to dance attendance on Annette. What had seemed a joke became serious. Aunt Nina, urged by Philip, remonstrated, and even the mamma of the pink sunbonnet began to look grave. It was all very well for a city demoiselle to talk with a fisherman and accept favours at his hands, provided that the city demoiselle understood that a vast and bridgeless gulf stretched between her and the fisherman. But when the demoiselle forgot the gulf and the fisherman refused to recognise it, why, it was time to take matters in hand.

To all of Aunt Nina's remonstrances, Philip's growlings, and the averted glances of her companions, Annette was deaf. "You are narrow-minded," she said laughingly. "I am interested in Monsieur LeConte simply as a study. He is entertaining. He talks well of his travels, and as for refusing to recognise the difference between us,why, he never dreamed of such a thing."

Suddenly a peremptory summons home from Annette's father put an end to the fears of Philip. Annette pouted, but papa must be obeyed. She blamed Philip and Aunt Nina for telling tales, but Aunt Nina was uncommunicative, and Philip too obviously cheerful to derive much satisfaction from.

That night she walked with the fisherman hand in hand on the sands. The wind from the pines bore the scarcely recognisable, subtle freshness of early autumn, and the waters had a hint of dying summer in their sob on the beach.

"You will remember," said the fisherman, "that I

have told you nothing about myself."

"Yes," murmured Annette.

"And you will keep your promises to me >"

"Yes."

"Let me hear you repeat them again."

"I promise you that I will not forget you. I promise you that I will never speak of you to anyone until I see you again. I promise that I will then clasp your hand wherever you may be."

"And mademoiselle will not be discouraged, but will continue her studies?"

"Yes."

It was all very romantic, by the waves of the Sound, under a harvest moon, that seemed all sympathy for these two, despite the fact that it was probably looking down upon hundreds of other equally romantic couples. Annette went to bed with glowing cheeks, and a heart whose pulsations would have caused a physician to prescribe unlimited digitalis.

It was still hot in New Orleans when she returned home, and it seemed hard to go immediately to work But if one is going to be an opera-singer someday and capture the world with one's voice, there is nothing to do but to study, study, sing, practise, even though one's throat be parched, one's head a great ache, and one's heart a nest of discouragement and sadness at what seems the uselessness of it all. Annette had now a new incentive to work. The fisherman had once praised her voice when she hummed a barcarole on the sands, and he had insisted that there was power in its rich notes. Though the fisherman had showed no cause why he should be accepted as a musical critic, Annette had somehow respected his judgment and been accordingly elated.

It was the night of the opening of the opera. There was the usual crush, the glitter and confusing radiance of the brilliant audience. Annette, with papa, Aunt Nina, and Philip, was late reaching her box. The curtain was up, and 'La Juive' was pouring forth defiance at her angry persecutors. Annette listened breathlessly. In fancy, she too was ringing her voice out to an applauding house. Her head unconsciously beat time to the music, and one hand half held her cloak from her bare shoulders.

Then Eleazar appeared, and the house rose at the end of his song. Encores it gave, and bravos and cheers. He bowed calmly, swept his eyes over the tiers until they found Annette, where they rested in a half-smile of recognition.

"Philip," gasped Annette, nervously raising her glasses, "my fisherman."

"Yes, an opera-singer is better than a merchant," drawled Philip.

The curtain fell on the first act. The house was won by the new tenor i it called and recalled him before the curtain. Clearly he had sung his way into the hearts of his audience at once.

"Papa, Aunt Nina," said Annette, "you must come behind the scenes with me. I want you to meet him. He is delightful. You must come."

Philip was bending ostentatiously over the girl in the next box. Papa and Aunt Nina consented to be dragged behind the scenes Annette was well known, for, in hopes of some day being an occupant of one of the dressing-rooms, she had made friends with everyone connected with the opera.

Eleazar received them, still wearing his brown garb and patriarchal beard.

"How you deceived me," she laughed, when the greetings and introductions were over.

"I came to America early," he smiled back at her, "and thought I'd try a little incognito at the Pass. I was not well, you see. It has been of great benefit to me."

"I kept my promise," she said in a lower tone.

"Thank you, that also has helped me."

Annette's teacher began to note a wonderful improvement in his pupil's voice. Never did a girl study so hard or practise so faithfully. It was truly wonderful. Now and then Annette would say to papa as if to reassure herself:

"And when Monsieur Cherbart says I am ready to go to Paris, may I go, papa?"

And papa would say a "Certainly" that would send her back to the piano with renewed ardour.

As for Monsieur LeConte, he was the idol of New Orleans. Seldom had there been a tenor who had sung himself so completely into the very hearts of a populace. When he was billed, the opera displayed *Standing Room Only* signs, no matter what the other attractions in the city might be. Sometimes Monsieur LeConte delighted small audiences in Annette's parlour, when the hostess was in a perfect flutter of happiness. Not often, you know, for the leading tenor was in great demand at the homes of society queens.

"Do you know," said Annette, petulantly, one evening, "I wish for the old days at Pass Christian."

"So do I," he answered tenderly, "will you repeat them with me next summer?"

"If I only could," she gasped.

Still she might have been happy, had it not been for Madame Dubeau the flute-voiced leading soprano, who wore the single dainty curl on her forehead, and thrilled her audiences oftentimes more completely than the fisherman. Madame Dubeau was La Juive to his Eleazar, Leonore to his Manfred, Elsa to his Lohengrin, Aida to his Rhadames, Marguerite to his Faust. In brief, Madame Dubeau was his opposite. She caressed him as Mignon, pleaded with him as Michaela, died for him in 'Les Huguenots,' broke her heart for love of him in 'La Favorite.' How could he help but love her, Annette asked herself, how could he? Madame Dubeau was beautiful and gifted and charming.

Once she whispered her fears to him when there was the meagrest bit of an opportunity. He laughed. "You don't understand, little one," he said tenderly, "the relations of professional people to each other are peculiar. After you go to Paris, you will know."

Still, New Orleans had built up its romance, and gossiped accordingly.

"Have you heard the news?" whispered Lola to Annette, leaning from her box at the opera one night. The curtain had just gone up on 'Herodias,' and for some reason or other, the audience applauded with more warmth than usual. There was a noticeable number of good-humoured, benignant smiles on the faces of the applauders.

"No," answered Annette, breathlessly, "no, indeed, Lola. I am going to Paris next week. I am so delighted I can't stop to think."

"Yes, that is excellent," said Lola, "but all New Orleans is smiling at the romance. Monsieur LeConte and Madame Dubeau were quietly married last night, but it leaked out this afternoon. See all the applause she's receiving."

Annette leaned back in her chair, very white and still. Her box was empty after the first act, and a quiet little tired voice that was almost too faint to be heard in the carriage on the way home, said:

"Papa, I don't think I care to go to Paris, after all."

M'SIEU FORTIER'S VIOLIN

SLOWLY, one by one, the lights in the French Opera go out, until there is but a single glimmer of pale yellow flickering in the great dark space, a few moments ago all a-glitter with jewels and the radiance of womanhood and a-clash with music. Darkness now, and silence, and a great haunted hush over all, save for the distant cheery voice of a stage hand humming a bar of the opera.

The glimmer of gas makes a halo about the bowed white head of«a little old man putting his violin carefully away in its case with aged, trembling, nervous fingers. Old M'sieu Fortier was the last one out every night.

Outside the air was murky, foggy. Gas and electricity were but faint splotches of light on the thick curtain of fog and mist. Around the opera was a mighty bustle of carriages and drivers and footmen, with a car gaining headway in the street now and then, a howling of names and numbers, the laughter and small talk of cloaked society stepping slowly to its carriages, and the more bourgeoisie vocalisation of the foot passengers who streamed along and hummed little bits of music. The fog's denseness was confusing, too, and at one moment it seemed that the little narrow street would become inextricably choked and remain so until some mighty engine would blow the crowd into atoms. It had been a crowded night. From around Toulouse Street, where led the entrance to the troisièmes, from the grand stairway, from the entrance to the quatrièmes, the human stream poured into the street, nearly all with a song on their lips.

M'sieu Fortier stood at the corner, blinking at the beautiful ladies in their carriages. He exchanged a hearty salutation with the saloon-keeper at the corner, then, tenderly carrying his violin case, he trudged down Bourbon Street, a little old, bent, withered figure, with shoulders shrugged up to keep warm, as though the faded brown overcoat were not thick enough.

Down on Bayou Road, not so far from Claiborne Street, was a house, little and old and queer, but quite large enough to hold M'sieu Fortier, a wrinkled dame, and a white cat. He was home but little, for on nearly every day there were rehearsals, then on Tuesday, Thursday, and Saturday nights, and twice Sundays there were performances, so Ma'am Jeanne and the white cat kept house almost always alone.

Then, when M'sieu Fortier was at home, why, it was practice, practice all the day, and smoke, snore, sleep at night. Altogether it was not very exhilarating.

M'sieu Fortier had played first violin in the orchestra ever since — well, no one remembered his not playing there. Sometimes there would come breaks in the seasons, and for a year the great building would be dark and silent. Then M'sieu Fortier would do jobs of playing here and there, one night for this ball, another night for that *soirée dansante* and, in the day, work at his trade, that of a cigar-maker. But now for seven years there had been no break in the season, and the little old violinist was happy. There is nothing sweeter than a regular job and good music to play, music into which one can put some soul, some expression, and which one must study to understand. Dance music, of the frivolous, frothy kind deemed essential to soirees, is trivial, easy, uninteresting.

So M'sieu Fortier, Ma'am Jeanne, and the white cat lived a peaceful, uneventful existence out on Bayou Road. When the opera season was over in February, M'sieu went back to cigar-making, and the white cat purred none the less contentedly.

It had been a benefit tonight for the leading tenor,

and he had chosen 'Roland a Ronceveaux,' a favourite this season, for his farewell. And, mon Dieu, mused the little M'sieu, but how his voice had rung out bell-like, piercing above the chorus of the first act. Encore after encore was given, and the bravos of the troisièmes were enough to stir the most sluggish of pulses.

Superbes Pyrenees
Qui dressez dans le ciel,
D'un hiver eternelle,
Pour nous livrer passage
Ouvrez vos larges flancs,
Faites taire l'orage,

M'sieu quickened his pace down Bourbon Street as he sang the chorus to himself in a thin old voice, and then, before he could see in the thick fog, he had run into two young men.

"I beg your pardon messieurs," he stammered.

"Most certainly," was the careless response, then the speaker, taking a second glance at the object of the rencontre, cried joyfully:

"Oh, M'sieu Fortier, is it you? Why, you are so happy, singing your love sonnet to your lady's eyebrow, that you didn't see a thing but the moon, did you? And who is the fair one who should clog your senses so?"

There was a deprecating shrug from the little man.

"*Ma foi*, but monsieur must know for sure, that I am too old for love songs."

"I know nothing save that I want that violin of yours. When is it to be mine, M'sieu Fortier?"

"Never, never," exclaimed M'sieu, gripping on as tightly to the case as if he feared it might be wrenched from him. "Me a lover, and to sell *mon* violin. Ah, so very foolish."

"Martel," said the first speaker to his companion as they moved on up town, "I wish you knew that little Frenchman. He's a unique specimen. He has the most exquisite violin I've seen in years; beautiful and mellow as a genuine Cremona, and he can make the music leap, sing, laugh, sob, skip, wail, anything you like from under his bow when he wishes. It's something wonderful. We are good friends. Picked him up in my French-town rambles. I've been trying to buy that instrument since—"

"To throw it aside a week later?" lazily inquired Martel. "You are like the rest of these modern day vandals, you can see nothing picturesque that you do not wish to deface for a souvenir. You cannot even let simple happiness alone, but must needs destroy it in a vain attempt to make it your own or parade it as an advertisement."

As for M'sieu Fortier, he went right on with his song and turned into Bayou Road, his shoulders still shrugged high as though he were cold, and into the quaint little house, where Ma'am Jeanne and the white cat, who always waited up for him at nights, were both nodding over the fire.

It was not long after this that the opera closed, and M'sieu went back to his old out-of-season job. But somehow he did not do as well this spring and summer as always. There is a certain amount of cunning and finesse required to roll a cigar just so, that M'sieu seemed to be losing, whether from age or deterioration it was hard to tell. Nevertheless, there was just about half as much money coming in as formerly, and the quaint little pucker between M'sieu's eyebrows which served for a frown came oftener and stayed longer than ever before.

"Minesse," he said one day to the white cat. He told all his troubles to her; it was of no use to talk to Ma'am Jeanne, she was too deaf to understand. "Minesse, we are getting poor. Your *père* git old, and his hands they go no mo' *rapidement,* and there be no mo' soirées these days. Minesse, if *la saison* don't hurry up, we shall eat very little meat."

And Minesse curled her tail and purred.

Before the summer had fairly begun, strange rumours began to float about in musical circles. M. Mauge would no longer manage the opera, but it would be turned into the hands of Americans, a syndicate. Bah! These English speaking people could do nothing unless there was a trust, a syndicate, a company immense and dishonest. It was going to be a guarantee business, with a strictly financial basis. But worse than all this, the new manager, who was now in France, would not only procure the artists, but a new orchestra, a new leader. M'sieu Fortier grew apprehensive at this, for he knew what the loss of his place would mean to him.

September and October came, and the papers were filled with accounts of the new artists from France and of the new orchestra leader too. He was described as a most talented, progressive, energetic young man. M'sieu Fortier's heart sank at the word 'progressive.' He was anything but that.

The New Orleans Creole blood flowed too sluggishly in his old veins.

November came, the opera reopened. M'sieu Fortier was not re-engaged.

"Minesse," he said with a catch in his voice that strongly resembled a sob, "Minesse, we must go hungry some time. Ah, *mon pauvre* violin. Ah, *mon Dieu*, they put us out, and they will not have us. Never mind, we will sing anyhow." And drawing his bow across the strings, he sang in his thin, quavering voice, "*Salut demeure, chaste et pure.*"

It is strange what a peculiar power of fascination former haunts have for the human mind. The criminal, after he has fled from justice, steals back and skulks about the scene of his crime; the employee thrown from work hangs about the place of his former industry; the schoolboy, truant or expelled, peeps in at the school-gate and taunts the good boys within. M'sieu Fortier was no exception. Night after night of the performances he climbed the stairs of the opera and sat, an attentive listener to the orchestra, with one ear inclined to the stage, and a quizzical expression on his wrinkled face. Then he would go home, and pat Minesse, and fondle the violin.

"Ah, Minesse, those new players! Not one bit can they play. Such tones, Minesse, such tones. All the time portemento, oh, so very bad. Ah, *mon chere* violin, we can play."

And he would play and sing a romance, and smile tenderly to himself.

At first it used to be into the deuxièmes that M'sieu Fortier went, into the front seats. But soon they were too expensive, and after all, one could hear just as well in the fourth row as in the first. After a while even the rear row of the deuxièmes was too costly, and the little musician wended his way with the plebeians around on Toulouse Street, and climbed the long, tedious flight of stairs into the troisièmes It makes no difference to be one row higher. It was more to the liking, after all. One felt more at home up here among the people. If one was thirsty, one could drink a glass of wine or beer being passed about by the libretto boys, and the music sounded just as well.

But it happened one night that M'sieu could not even afford to climb the Toulouse Street stairs. To be sure, there was yet another gallery, the quatrièmes, where the peanut boys went for a dime, but M'sieu could not get down to that yet. So he stayed outside until all the beautiful women in their warm wraps, a bright-hued chattering throng, came down the grand staircase to their carriages.

It was on one of these nights that Courcey and

Martel found him shivering at the corner.

"Hello, M'sieu Fortier," cried Courcey, "are you ready to let me have that violin yet?"

"For shame," interrupted Martel.

"Fifty dollars, you know," continued Courcey, taking no heed of his friend's interpolation.

M'sieu Fortier made a courtly bow. "If Monsieur will call at my house tomorrow, he may have mon violin," he said huskily, then turned abruptly on his heel, and went down Bourbon Street, his shoulders drawn high as though he were cold.

When Courcey and Martel entered the gate of the little house on Bayou Road the next day, there floated out to their ears music from the violin, that told more than speech or tears or gestures could have done of the utter sorrow and desolation of the little old man. They walked softly up the short red brick path and tapped at the door. Within, M'sieu Fortier was caressing the violin, with silent tears streaming down his wrinkled gray face.

There was not much said on either side. Courcey came away with the instrument, leaving the money behind, while Martel grumbled at the essentially sordid, mercenary spirit of the world. M'sieu Fortier turned back into the room, after bowing his visitors out with old time French courtliness, and turning to the sleepy white cat, said with a dry sob:

"Minesse, there's only me and you now."

About six days later, Courcey's morning dreams were disturbed by the announcement of a visitor. Hastily doing a toilet, he descended the stairs to find M'sieu Fortier nervously pacing the hall floor.

"I come to bring back your money, yes. I cannot sleep, I cannot eat, I only cry, and think, and wish for mon violin; and Minesse, and the old woman too, they mope and look bad too, all for mon violin. I try to use that money, but it burn and sting like blood money. I feel like I done sold my child. I cannot go at l'opera no mo', I t'ink of mon violin. I starve before I live without. My heart, he is broke, I die for mon violin."

Courcey left the room and returned with the instrument.

"M'sieu Fortier," he said, bowing low, as he handed the case to the little man, "take your violin. It was a whim with me, a passion with you. And as for the money, why, keep that too. It was worth a hundred dollars to have possessed such an instrument even for six days."

BY THE BAYOU ST. JOHN

THE Bayou St. John slowly makes its dark-hued way through reeds and rushes, high banks and flat slopes, until it casts itself into the turbulent bosom of Lake Pontchartrain. It is dark, like the passionate women of Egypt; placid, like their broad brows; deep, silent, like their souls. Within its bosom are hidden romances and stories, such as were sung by minstrels of old. From the source to the mouth is not far distant, visibly speaking, but in the life of the bayou a hundred heart-miles could scarce measure it. Just where it winds about the northwest of the city are some of its most beautiful bits, orange groves on one side, and quaint old Spanish gardens on the other.

Who cares that the bridges are modern, and that here and there pert boat-houses rear their prim heads? It is the bayou, even though it be invaded with the ruthless vandalism of the improving idea, and can a boat-house kill the beauty of a moss-grown centurion of an oak with a history as old as the city? Can an iron bridge with tarantula piers detract from the song of a mockingbird in a fragrant orange grove? We know that farther out, past the Confederate Soldiers' Home — that rose-embowered, rambling place of gray-coated, white-haired old men with broken hearts for a lost cause — it flows, unimpeded by the faintest conception of man, and we love it all the more that, like the Priestess of Isis, it is calm-browed, even in indignity.

To its banks at the end of Moss Street, one day there came a man and a maiden. They were both tall and lithe and slender, with the agility of youth and fire. He was the final concentration of the essence of Spanish passion filtered into an American frame. She, a repressed Southern exotic, trying to fit itself into the niches of a modern civilisation. Truly, a fitting couple to seek the bayou banks.

They climbed the levee that stretched a feeble check to waters that seldom rise, and on the other side of the embankment, at the brink of the river, she sat on a log, and impatiently pulled off the little cap she wore. The skies were gray, heavy, overcast, with an occasional wind-rift in the clouds that only revealed new depths of grayness behind. The tideless waters murmured a faint ripple against the logs and jutting beams of the breakwater, and were answered by the crescendo wail of the dried reeds on the other bank that rustled and moaned among themselves for the golden days of summer sunshine.

He stood up, his dark form a slender silhouette against the sky. She looked upward from her log, and their eyes met with an exquisite shock of recognising understanding; dark eyes into dark eyes, Iberian fire into Iberian fire, soul unto soul: it was enough. He sat down and took her into his arms, and in the eerie murmur of the storm coming they talked of the future.

"And then I hope to go to Italy or France. It is only there, beneath those far Southern skies, that I could ever hope to attain to anything that the soul within me says I can. I have wasted so much time in the mere struggle for bread, while the powers of a higher calling have clamoured for recognition and expression. I will go some day and redeem myself."

She was silent a moment, watching with half-closed lids a dejected-looking hunter on the other bank, and a lean dog who trailed through the reeds behind him with drooping tail. Then she asked:

"And I, what will become of me?"

"You, Athanasia? There is a great future before you, little woman, and I and my love can only mar it. Try to forget me and go your way. I am only the epitome of unhappiness and bad luck."

But she laughed and would have none of it.

Will you ever forget that day, Athanasia? How the little gamins, Creole throughout, came half shyly near the log, fishing, and exchanging furtive whispers and half-concealed glances at the silent couple. Their angling was rewarded only by a little black watermoccasin that wriggled and forked its venomous red tongue in an attempt to exercise its death-dealing prerogative. This Athanasia insisted must go back into its native black waters, and paid the price the boys asked that it might enjoy its freedom. The gamins laughed and chattered in their soft patois; the Don smiled tenderly upon Athanasia, and she durst not look at the reeds as she talked, lest their crescendo sadness yield a foreboding. Just then a wee girl appeared, clad in a multi-hued garment, evidently a sister to the small fishermen. Her keen black eyes set in a dusky face glanced sharply and suspiciously at the group as she clambered over the wet embankment, and it seemed the drizzling mist grew colder, the sobbing wind more pronounced in its prophetic wail. Athanasia rose suddenly. "Let us go," she said, "the eternal feminine has spoiled it all."

The bayou flows as calmly, as darkly, as full of hidden passions as ever. On a night years after, the moon was shining upon it with a silvery tenderness that seemed brighter, more caressingly lingering than anywhere within the old city. Behind, there rose the spires and towers; before, only the reeds, green now, and soft in their rustlings and whisperings for the future. False reeds. They tell themselves of their happiness to be, and it all ends in dry stalks and drizzling skies. The mocking-bird in the fragrant orange grove sends out his night song, and blends it with the cricket's chirp, as the blossoms of orange and magnolia mingle their perfume with the earthy smell of a summer rain just blown over. Perfect in its stillness, absolute in its beauty, tenderly healing in its suggestion of peace, the night in its clear-lighted, cloudless sweetness enfolds Athanasia, as she stands on the levee and gazes down at the old log, now almost hidden in the luxuriant grass.

"It was the eternal feminine that spoiled our dream that day as it spoiled the after life, was it not?"

But the Bayou St. John did not answer. It merely gathered into its silent bosom another broken-hearted romance, and flowed dispassionately on its way.

WHEN THE BAYOU OVERFLOWS

WHEN the sun goes down behind the great oaks along the Bayou Teche near Franklin, it throws red needles of light into the dark woods, and leaves a great glow on the still bayou.

Ma'am Mouton paused at her gate and cast a contemplative look at the red sky.

"It will rain tomorrow. I must git in my things."

She moved briskly about the yard, taking things from the line, when Louisette's voice called cheerily:

"Ah, Ma'am Mouton, can I help?"

Louisette was petite and plump and black-haired. Louisette's eyes danced, and her lips were red and tempting. Ma'am Mouton's face relaxed as the small brown hands relieved hers of their burden.

"Sylves', has he come yet?" asked the red mouth.

"*Mais non, ma chere,*" said Ma'am Mouton, sadly, "I can't tell why he no come home soon these days. I feel like something going happen. He so strange."

Even as she spoke a quick nervous step was heard up the brick path. Sylves' paused an instant without the kitchen door, his face turned to the setting sun. He was tall and slim and agile; a true cajun.

"*Bonjour,* Louisette," he laughed. "Eh, maman."

"Ah, my son, you are very late."

Sylves' frowned, but said nothing. It was a silent supper that followed,

Louisette was sad, Ma'am Mouton sighed now and then, Sylves' was constrained.

"Maman," he said at length, "I am going away."

Ma'am Mouton dropped her fork and stared at him with unseeing eyes. Then, as she comprehended his remark, she put her hand out to him with a pitiful gesture.

"Sylves'," cried Louisette, springing to her feet.

"Maman, don't, don't," he said weakly, then gathering strength from the silence, he burst forth:

"Yes, I'm going away to work. I'm tired of dis, jus' dig, dig, work in the field, nothing to see but the cloud, the tree, the bayou. I don't like New Orleans. It too near here, there's no mo' money there. I go up to Mardi Gras, and it's the same people, the same streets. I'm going to Chicago."

"Sylves'!" screamed both women at once.

Chicago! That vast, far-off city that seemed in another world. Chicago! A name to conjure with for wickedness.

"Why, yes," continued Sylves', "lots of boys I know there. Henri and Joseph Lascaud and Arthur, they write me what money they make in cigars. I can make a living too. I can make fine cigars. See how I do in New Orleans in the winter."

"Oh, Sylves'," wailed Louisette, "then you'll forget me."

"Non, non, ma chere," he answered tenderly. "I will come back when the bayou overflows again, and maman and Louisette will have fine present."

Ma'am Mouton had bowed her head on her hands, and was rocking to and fro in an agony of dry-eyed misery.

Sylves' went to her side and knelt.

"Maman," he said softly, "maman, you must not cry. All te boys go away. I will come back, and when I do you won't have to work no mo'."

But Ma'am Mouton was inconsolable.

It was even as Sylves' had said. In the summertime the boys of the Bayou Teche would work in the field or in the town of Franklin, hack-driving and doing odd jobs. When winter came, there was a general exodus to New Orleans, a hundred miles away, where work was to be had as cigarmakers. There is money, plenty of it, in cigar-making, if one can get in the right place. Of late, however, there had been a general slackness of the trade. Last winter oftentimes Sylves' had walked the streets out of work. Many were the Creole boys who had gone to Chicago to earn a living, for the cigar-making trade flourishes there wonderfully. Friends of Sylves' had gone, and written home glowing accounts of the money to be had almost for the asking. When one's blood leaps for new scenes, new adventures, and one needs money, what is the use of frittering away time alternately between the Bayou Teche and New Orleans? Sylves' had brooded all summer, and now that September had come, he was determined to go.

Louisette, the orphan, the girl-lover, whom everyone in Franklin knew would some day be Ma'am Mouton's daughter-in-law, wept and pleaded in vain. Sylves' kissed her quivering.

"Ma chere," he would say, "t'ink, I will bring you one fine diamond ring, next spring, when the bayou overflows again."

Louisette would fain be content with this promise. As for Ma'am Mouton, she seemed to have grown ages older.

Her Sylves' was going from her. Sylves', whose trips to New Orleans had been a yearly source of heartbreak, was going far away for months to that mistily wicked city, a thousand miles away.

October came, and Sylves' had gone. Ma'am Mouton had kept up bravely until the last, when with one final cry she extended her arms to the pitiless train bearing him northward. Then she and Louisette went home drearily, the one leaning upon the other.

Ah, that was a great day when the first letter came from Chicago. Louisette came running in breathlessly from the post-office, and together they read it again and again. Chicago was such a wonderful city, said Sylves'. Why, it was always like New Orleans at Mardi Gras with the people. He had seen Joseph Lascaud, and he had a place to work promised him. He was not well, but he wanted, oh, so much, to see maman and Louisette. But then, he could wait.

Was ever such a wonderful letter? Louisette sat for an hour afterwards building gorgeous air-castles, while Ma'am Mouton fingered the paper and murmured prayers to the Virgin for Sylves'. When the bayou overflowed again? That would be in April. Then Louisette caught herself looking critically at her slender brown fingers, and blushed furiously, though Ma'am Mouton could not see her in the gathering twilight.

Next week there was another letter, even more wonderful than the first. Sylves' had found work. He was making cigars, and was earning two dollars a day. Such wages. Ma'am Mouton and Louisette began to plan pretty things for the brown cottage on the Teche.

That was a pleasant winter, after all. True, there was no Sylves', but then he was always in New Orleans for a few months any way. There were his letters, full of wondrous tales of the great queer city, where cars went by ropes underground, and where there was no Mardi Gras and the people did not mind Lent. Now and then there would be a present, a keepsake for Louisette, and some money for maman. They would plan improvements for the cottage, and Louisette began to do sewing and dainty crochet, which she would hide with a blush if anyone hinted at a trousseau.

It was March now, and Spring time. The bayou began to sweep down between its banks less sluggishly than before. It was rising, and soon would spread over its tiny levees. The doors could be left open now, though the trees were not yet green. But then down here the trees do not swell and bud slowly and tease you for weeks with promises of greenness. Dear no, they simply look mysterious, and their twigs shake against each other and tell secrets of the leaves that will soon be born. Then one morning you awake and, lo and behold, it is a green world. The boughs have suddenly clothed themselves all in a wondrous garment, and you feel the blood run riot in your veins out of pure sympathy.

One day in March, it was warm and sweet. Underfoot were violets, and wee white star flowers peering through the baby-grass. The sky was blue, with flecks of white clouds reflecting themselves in the brown bayou. Louisette tripped up the red brick walk with the Chicago letter in her hand, and paused a minute at the door to look upon the leaping waters, her eyes dancing.

"I know the bayou must be ready to overflow," went the letter in the carefully phrased French that the brothers taught at the parochial school, "and I am glad, for I want to see the dear maman and my Louisette. I am not so well, and Monsieur le docteur says it is well for me to go to the South again."

Monsieur le docteur, Sylves' not well! The thought struck a chill to the hearts of Ma'am Mouton and Louisette, but not for long. Of course, Sylves' was not well He was also homesick; it was to be expected.

At last the great day came, Sylves' would be home. The brown waters of the bayou had spread until they were seemingly trying to rival the Mississippi in width. The little house was scrubbed and cleaned until it shone again. Louisette had looked her dainty little dress over and over to be sure that there was not a flaw to be found wherein Sylves' could compare her unfavourably to the stylish Chicago girls.

The train rumbled in on the platform, and two pair of eyes opened wide for the first glimpse of Sylves'. The porter, all officiousness and brass buttons, bustled up to Ma'am Mouton.

"This is Mrs. Mouton?" he inquired deferentially.

Ma'am Mouton nodded, her heart sinking. "Where is Sylves'?"

"He is here, madam."

There appeared Joseph Lascaud, then some men bearing Something. Louisette put her hands up to her eyes to hide the sight, but Ma'am Mouton was rigid.

"It was too cold for him," Joseph was saying to almost deaf ears, "and he took the consumption. He thought he could get well when he come home. He talk all the way down about the bayou, and about you and Louisette. But he had a bad haemorrhage, and he died from weakness. Just three hours ago. He said he wanted to get home and give Louisette her diamond ring, when the bayou overflowed."

ODALIE

Now and then Carnival time comes at the time of the good Saint Valentine, and then sometimes it comes as late as the warm days in March, when spring is indeed upon us, and the greenness of the grass outvies the green in the royal standards.

Days and days before the Carnival proper, New Orleans begins to take on a festive appearance. Here and there the royal flags with their glowing greens and violets and yellows appear, and then, as if by magic, the streets and buildings flame and burst like poppies out of bud, into a glorious refulgence of colour that steeps the senses into a languorous acceptance of warmth and beauty.

On Mardi Gras day, as you know, it is a town gone mad with folly. A huge masked ball emptied into the streets at daylight; a meeting of all nations on common ground, a pot-pourri of every conceivable human ingredient, but faintly describes it all. There are music and flowers, cries and laughter and song and joyousness, and never an aching heart to show its sorrow or dim the happiness of the streets. A wondrous thing, this Carnival.

But the old cronies down in Frenchtown, who

know everything, and can recite you many a story, tell of one sad heart on Mardi Gras years ago. It was a woman's, of course, for '*Il est toujours les femmes qui sont malheureuses,*' says an old proverb, and perhaps it is right. This woman — a child, she would be called elsewhere, save in this land of tropical growth and precocity — lost her heart to one who never knew, a very common story, by the way, but one which would have been quite distasteful to the haughty judge, her father, had he known.

Odalie was beautiful. Odalie was haughty too, but gracious enough to those who pleased her dainty fancy. In the old French house on Royal Street, with its quaint windows and Spanish courtyard green and cool, and made musical by the splashing of the fountain and the trill of caged birds, lived Odalie in convent-like seclusion. Monsieur le Juge was determined no hawk should break through the cage and steal his dove. And so, though there was no mother, a stern aunt kept faithful watch.

Alas for the precautions of la Tante. Bright eyes that search for other bright eyes in which lurks the spirit of youth and mischief are ever on the lookout, even in church. Dutifully was Odalie marched to the Cathedral every Sunday to mass, and Tante Louise, nodding devoutly over her beads, could not see the blushes and glances full of meaning, a whole code of signals as it were, that passed between Odalie and Pierre, the impecunious young clerk in the courtroom.

Odalie loved, perhaps, because there was not much else to do. When one is shut up in a great French house with a grim sleepy tante and no companions of one's own age, life becomes a dull thing, and one is ready for any new sensation, particularly if in the veins there bounds the tempestuous Spanish-French blood that Monsieur le Juge boasted of. So Odalie hugged the image of her Pierre during the week days, and played tremulous little lovesongs to it in the twilight when la Tante dozed over her devotion book, and on Sundays at mass there were glances and blushes, and perhaps, at some especially remembered time, the touch of fingertips at the holy water font, while la Tante dropped her last genuflexion.

Then came the Carnival time, and one little heart beat faster, as the gray house on Royal Street hung out its many-hued flags, and draped its grim front with glowing colours. It was to be a time of joy and relaxation, when everyone could go abroad, and in the crowds one could speak to whom one chose. Unconscious plans formulated, and the petite Odalie was quite happy as the time drew near.

"Only think, Tante Louise," she would cry, "what a happy time it is to be."

But Tante Louise only grumbled, as was her wont.

It was Mardi Gras day at last, and early through her window Odalie could hear the jingle of folly bells on the maskers' costumes, the tinkle of music, and the echoing strains of songs. Up to her ears there floated the laughter of the older maskers, and the screams of the little children frightened at their own images under the mask and domino. What a hurry to be out and in the motley merry throng, to be pacing Royal Street to Canal Street, where was life and the world.

They were tired eyes with which Odalie looked at the gay pageant at last, tired with watching throng after throng of maskers, of the unmasked, of peering into the cartsful of singing minstrels, into carriages of revellers, hoping for a glimpse of Pierre the devout. The allegorical carts rumbling by with their important red-clothed horses were beginning to lose charm, the disguises showed tawdry, even the gay-hued flags fluttered sadly to Odalie.

Mardi Gras was a tiresome day, after all, she

sighed, and Tante Louise agreed with her for once.

Six o'clock had come, the hour when all masks must be removed. The long red rays of the setting sun glinted athwart the many-hued costumes of the revellers trooping unmasked homeward to rest for the night's last mad frolic.

Down Toulouse Street there came the merriest throng of all. Young men and women in dainty, fairy-like garb, dancers, and dresses of the picturesque Empire, a butterfly or two and a dame here and there with powdered hair and graces of olden time. Singing with unmasked faces, they danced toward Tante Louise and Odalie. She stood with eyes lustrous and tear-heavy, for there in the front was Pierre, Pierre the faithless, his arms about the slender waist of a butterfly, whose tinselled.powdered hair floated across the lace ruffles of his Empire coat.

"Pierre," cried Odalie, softly. No one heard, for it was a mere faint breath and fell unheeded. Instead the laughing throng pelted her with flowers and candy and went their way, and even Pierre did not see.

You see, when one is shut up in the grim walls of a Royal Street house, with no one but a Tante Louise and a grim judge, how is one to learn that in this world there are faithless ones who may glance tenderly into one's eyes at mass and pass the holy water on caressing fingers without being madly in love? There was no one to tell Odalie, so she sat at home in the dull first days of Lent, and nursed her dear dead love, and mourned as women have done from time immemorial over the faithlessness of man. And when one day she asked that she might go back to the Ursulines' convent where her childish days were spent, only to go this time as a nun, Monsieur le Juge and Tante Louise thought it quite the proper and convenient thing to do, for how were they to know the secret of that Mardi Gras day?

LA JUANITA

IF YOU never lived in Mandeville you cannot appreciate the thrill of wholesome, satisfied joy which sweeps over its inhabitants every evening at five o'clock. It is the hour for the arrival of the 'New Camelia,' the happening of the day. As early as four o'clock the trailing smoke across the horizon of the treacherous Lake Pontchartrain appears, and Mandeville knows then that the hour for its siesta has passed, and that it must array itself in its coolest garments, and go down to the pier to meet this sole connection between itself and the outside world; the little, puffy, side-wheel steamer that comes daily from New Orleans and brings the mail and the news.

On this particular day there was an air of suppressed excitement about the people gathered on the pier. To be sure, there were no outward signs to show that anything unusual had occurred. The small folks danced with the same glee over the worn boards, and peered down with daring excitement into the perilous depths of the water below. The sun, fast sinking in a gorgeous glow behind the pines of the Tchefuncta region far away, danced his mischievous rays in much the same manner that he

did every other day. But there was a something in the
air, a something not tangible, but mysterious, subtle.
You could catch an indescribable whiff of it in your
inner senses, by the half-eager, furtive glances that
the small crowd cast at La Juanita.

"*Gar, gar, le bateau,*" said one dark-tressed mother
to the wide-eyed baby. "*Et, oui,*" she added, in an
undertone to her companion. "*Voila, La Juanita.*"

La Juanita, you must know, was the pride of
Mandeville, the adored, the admired of all, with her
petite, half-Spanish, half-French beauty. Whether
rocking in the shade of the Cherokeerose-covered
gallery of Grandpère Colomes' big house, her fair
face bonnet-shaded, her dainty hands gloved to keep
the sun from too close an acquaintance, or splashing
the spray from the bow of her little pirogue, or
fluffing her skirts about her tiny feet on the pier, she
was the pet and ward of Mandeville, as it were, La
Juanita Alvarez, since Madame Alvarez was a widow,
and Grandpère Colomes was strict and stern.

Now La Juanita had set her small foot down with
a passionate stamp before Grandpère Colomes' very
face, and tossed her black curls about her wilful head,
and said she would go to the pier this evening to
meet her Mercer. All Mandeville knew this, and cast

its furtive glances alternately at La Juanita with two big pink spots in her cheeks, and at the entrance to the pier, expecting Grandpère Colomes and a scene.

The sun cast red glows and violet shadows over the pier, and the pines murmured a soft little vesper hymn among themselves up on the beach, as the 'New Camelia' swung herself in, crabby, sidewise, like a fat old gentleman going into a small door. There was the clang of an important bell, the scream of a hoarse little whistle, and Mandeville rushed to the gang-plank to welcome the outside world. Juanita put her hand through a waiting arm, and tripped away with her Mercer, big and blond and brawny. "Un Americain, pah!" said the little mother of the black eyes. And Mandeville sighed sadly, and shook its head, and was sorry for Grandpère Colomes.

This was Saturday, and the big regatta would be Monday. There were to be boats from Madisonville and Amite, from Lewisburg and Covington, and even far-away Nott's Point. There was to be a Class A and Class B and Class C, and the little French girls of the town flaunted their ribbons down the one oak-shaded, lake-kissed street, and dared anyone to say theirs were not the favourite colours.

In Class A was entered, " 'La Juanita,' captain

Mercer Grangeman, colours pink and gold."

Her name, her colours; what impudence!

Of course, not being a Mandevillian, you could not understand the shame of Grandpère Colomes at this. Was it not bad enough for his petite Juanita, his Spanish blossom, his hope of a family that had held itself proudly aloof from "dose Americain" from time immemorial, to have smiled upon this Mercer, this pale-eyed youth? Was it not bad enough for her to demean herself by walking upon the pier with him? But for a boat, his boat, "un bateau Americain," to be named La Juanita. Oh, the shame of it. Grandpère Colomes prayed a devout prayer to the Virgin that 'La Juanita' should be capsized.

Monday came, clear and blue and stifling. The waves of hot air danced on the sands and adown the one street merrily. Glassily calm lay the Pontchartrain, heavily still hung the atmosphere. Madame Alvarez cast an inquiring glance toward the sky. Grandpère Colomes chuckled. He had not lived on the shores of the treacherous Lake Pontchartrain for nothing. He knew its every mood, its petulances and passions. He knew this glassy warmth and what it meant. Chuckling again and again, he stepped to the gallery and looked out over the lake, and at the pier, where lay the boats rocking and idly tugging at their moorings. La Juanita in her rose-scented room tied the pink ribbons on her dainty frock, and fastened cloth of gold roses at her lithe waist.

It was said that just before the crack of the pistol La Juanita's tiny hand lay in Mercer's, and that he bent his head, and whispered softly, so that the surrounding crowd could not hear:

"Juanita mine, if I win, you will?"

"Oui, mon Mercere, if you win."

In another instant the white wings were off scudding before the rising breeze, dipping their glossy boat-sides into the clear water, straining their cordage in their tense efforts to reach the stake boats. Mandeville indiscriminately distributed itself on piers, large and small, bath-house tops, trees, and craft of all kinds, from pirogue, dory, and pine-raft to pretentious cat-boat and shell-schooner. Mandeville cheered and strained its eyes after all the boats, but chiefly was its attention directed to 'La Juanita.'

"*Ah, voila*, it is ahead."

"*Mais non, c'est un autre.*"

"*La Juanita. Regardez Grandpère Colomes.*"

Old Colomes on the big pier with Madame Alvarez and his granddaughter was intently straining his weather-beaten face in the direction of Nott's Point, his back resolutely turned upon the scudding white wings. A sudden chuckle of grim satisfaction caused La Petite's head to toss petulantly.

Only for a minute. Grandpère Colomes' chuckle was followed by a shout of dismay from those whose glance had followed his. You must know that it is around Nott's Point that the storm king shows his wings first, for the little peninsula guards the entrance which leads into the southeast waters of the stormy Rigolets and the blustering Gulf. You would know, if you lived in Mandeville, that when the pines on Nott's Point darken and when the water shows white beyond like the teeth of a hungry wolf, it is time to steer your boat into the mouth of one of the many calm bayous which flow silently throughout St. Tammany parish into the lake. Small wonder that the cry of dismay went up now, for Nott's Point was black, with a lurid light overhead, and the roar of the grim southeast wind came ominously over the water.

La Juanita clasped her hands and strained her eyes for her namesake.

The racers had rounded the second stake-boat, and the course of the triangle headed them directly for the lurid cloud.

You should have seen Grandpère Colomes then. He danced up and down the pier in a perfect frenzy. The thin pale lips of Madame Alvarez moved in a silent prayer. 'La Juanita' stood coldly silent.

The advance guard of the southeast force had struck the little fleet. They dipped and scurried and rocked, and you could see the sails being reefed hurriedly, and almost hear the rigging creak and moan under the strain. Then the wind came up the lake, and struck the town with a tumultuous force. The waters rose and heaved in the long, sullen ground-swell, which betokened serious trouble. There was a rush of lake-craft to shelter. Heavy gray waves boomed against the breakwaters and piers, dashing their brackish spray upon the strained watchers; then with a shriek and a howl the storm burst full, with blinding sheets of rain, and a great hurricane of Gulf wind that threatened to blow the little town away.

La Juanita was proud. When Grandpère and Madame led her away in the storm, though her face was white, and the rose mouth pressed close, not a word did she say, and her eyes were as bright as ever before. It was foolish to hope that the frail boats could survive such a storm. There was not even the merest excuse for shelter out in the waters, and when Lake Pontchartrain grows angry, it devours without pity.

Your tropical storm is soon over. In an hour the sun struggled through a gray and misty sky, over which the wind was sweeping great clouds. The rain-drops hung diamond-like on the thick foliage, but the long ground-swell still boomed against the breakwaters and showed white teeth, far to the south.

As chickens creep from under shelter after a rain, so the people of Mandeville crept out again on the piers and watched eagerly for the boats. Slowly upon the horizon appeared white sails, and the little craft swung into sight. One, two, three, four, five, six, seven, eight, nine, counted Mandeville. Every one coming in. Bravo! A great cheer swept the length of the town from the post-office to Black Bayou. Bravo! Every boat was coming in. But was every man?

This was a sobering thought, and in the hush which followed it you could hear the train thundering over the great lake-bridge, miles away.

Well, they came into the pier at last, 'La Juanita' in the lead; and as Captain Mercer landed, he was surrounded by a voluble, chattering, anxious throng that loaded him with questions in patois, in broken English, and in French. He was no longer "un

Americain" now, he was a hero.

When the other eight boats came in, and Mandeville saw that no one was lost, there was another ringing bravo, and more questions.

We heard the truth finally. When the storm burst, Captain Mercer suddenly promoted himself to an admiralship and assumed command of his little fleet. He had led them through the teeth of the gale to a small inlet on the coast between Bayou Lacombe and Nott's Point, and there they had waited until the storm passed. Loud were the praises of the other captains for Admiral Mercer, profuse were the thanks of the sisters and sweethearts, as he was carried triumphantly on the shoulders of the sailors adown the wharf to the Maison Colomes.

The crispness had gone from Juanita's pink frock, and the cloth of gold roses were wellnigh petalless, but the hand that she slipped into his was warm and soft, and the eyes that were upturned to Mercer's blue ones were shining with admiring tears. And even Grandpère Colomes, as he brewed on the Cherokee-rose-covered gallery, a fiery punch for the heroes, was heard to admit that "some time dose Americain can mos' be like one Frenchman."

We danced at the betrothal supper the next week.

THREE THOUGHTS

How few of us in all the world's great, ceaseless struggling strife, go to our work with gladsome, buoyant step, and love it for its sake, whatever it be. Because it is a labor, or perhaps some sweet, peculiar art of God's own gift, and not the promise of the world's slow smile of recognition, or of mammon's gilded grasp.

Alas how few in inspiration's dazzling flash, or spiritual sense of world's beyond the dome, of circling blue around this weary earth, can bask and know the God-given grace of genius' fire that flows and permeates the virgin mind alone, the soul in which the love of earth hath tainted not. The love of art and art alone.

"Who dares stand forth?" the monarch cried, "amid the throng, and dare to give their aid, and bid this wretch to live? I pledge my faith and crown beside, a woeful plight, a sorry sight, this outcast from all God-given grace. What ho, in all, no friendly face, no helping hand to stay his plight? St. Peter's name be pledged, the man's accursed, that is true; but ho, he suffers. None of you will mercy show, or pity sigh?"

Strong men drew back, and lordly train did slowly file from monarch's look, whose lips curled scorn. But from a nook a voice cried out, "Though he has slain that which I loved the best on earth, yet will I tend him till he dies. I can be brave." A woman's eyes gazed fearlessly into his own.

When all the world has grown full cold to thee, and man — proud pygmy — shrugs all scornfully and bitter, blinding tears flow gushing forth, because of thine own sorrows and poor plight, then turn ye swift to nature's page, and read there passions, immeasurably far greater than thine own in all their littleness. For nature has her sorrows and her joys, as all the piled-up mountains and low vales will silently attest. Hang thy head in dire confusion, for having dared to moan at thine own miseries when God and nature suffer silently.

A COMPLAINT

Dear God, it is hard, so awful hard to lose the one we love, and see him go afar, with scarce one thought of aching hearts behind, nor wistful eyes, nor outstretched yearning hands.

Chide not, dear God, if surging thoughts arise, and bitter questionings of love and fate. Rather give my weary heart thy rest and turn the sad, dark memories into sweet.

Dear God, I would my loved one were near, but since thou will'st that happy thence he'll be, I send him forth, and back I'll choke the grief. Rebellion rises in my lonely heart. I pray thee, God, my loved one joy to bring; I dare not hope that joy will be with me, but ah, dear God, one boon I crave of thee — that he shall never forget his hours with me.

IN UNCONSCIOUSNESS

There was a big booming in my ears, great heavy iron bells that swung to and fro on either side, and sent out deafening reverberations that steeped the senses in a musical melody of sonorous sound; to and fro, backward and forward, yet ever receding in a gradually widening circle, monotonous, mournful, weird, suffusing the soul with an unutterable sadness, as images of wailing processions, of weeping, empty-armed women, and widowed maidens flashed through the mind, and settled on the soul with a crushing, overpressing weight of sorrow.

Now I lay floating, arms outstretched, on an illimitable waste of calm tranquil waters. Far away as eye could reach, there was naught but the pale, whiteflecked, green waters of this ocean of eternity, and above the tender blue sky arched down in perfect love of its mistress, the ocean. Sky and sea, sea and sky, blue, calm, infinite, perfect sea, heaving its womanly bosom to the passionate kisses of its ardent sun-lover. Away into infinity stretched this perfectibility of love. Into eternity I was drifting alone, silent, yet burdened still with the remembrance of the sadness of the bells.

Far away, they tolled out the incessant dirge, grown resignedly sweet now; so intense in its infinite peace, that a calm of love, beyond all human understanding and above all earthly passions, sank deep into my soul, and so permeated my whole being with rest and peace, that my lips smiled and my eyes drooped in access of fulsome joy. Into the illimitable space of infinity we drifted, my soul and I, borne along only by the network of auburn hair that floated about me in the green waters.

But now, a rude grasp from somewhere is laid upon me, pressing upon my face. Instantly the air grows gloomy, gray, and the ocean rocks menacingly, while the great bells grow harsh and strident, as they hint of a dark fate. I clasp my hands appealingly to the heavens. I moan and struggle with the unknown grasp, then there is peace and the sweet content of the infinite Nirvana.

Then slowly, softly, the net of auburn hair begins to drag me down below the surface of the sea. Oh, the skies are so sweet, and now that the tender stars are looking upon us, how fair to stay and sway upon the breast of eternity. But the net is inexorable, and gently, slowly pulls me down. Now we sink straight, now we whirl in slow, eddying circles, spiral-like.

While at each turn those bells ring out clanging now in wild crescendo, then whispering dread secrets of the ocean's depths. Oh ye mighty bells, tell me from your learned lore of the hopes of mankind. Tell me what fruit he beareth from his strivings and yearnings. Know not ye? Why ring ye now so joyful, so hopeful, then toll your dismal prophecies of overcast skies?

Years have passed, and now centuries, too, are swallowed in the gulf of eternity, yet the auburn net still whirls me in eddying circles. Down to the very womb of time. To the innermost recesses of the mighty ocean.

And now, peace, perfect, unconditioned, sublime peace, and rest, and silence. For to the great depths of the mighty ocean the solemn bells cannot penetrate, and no sound, not even the beatings of one's own heart, is heard. In the heart of eternity there can be nothing to break the calm of frozen aeons. In the great white hall I lay, silent, unexpectant, calm, and smiled in perfect content at the web of auburn hair which trailed across my couch. No passionate longing for life or love, no doubting question of heaven or hell, no strife for carnal need. Only rest, content, peace, happiness, perfect, whole, complete, sublime.

And thus passed ages and ages, aeons and aeons. The great earth there in the dim distance above the ocean has toiled wearily about the sun, until its mechanism was failing, and the warm ardor of the lover's eye was becoming pale and cold from age, while the air all about the fast dwindling sphere was heavy and thick with the sorrows and heart-aches and woes of the humans upon its face. Heavy with the screams and roar of war, with the curses of the deceived of traitors, with the passionate sighs of unlawful love, with the crushing unrest of blighted hopes. Knowledge and contempt of all these things permeated even to the inmost depths of time, as I lay in the halls of rest and smiled at the web floating through my white fingers.

But hark, discord begins. There is a vague fear which springs from an unknown source and drifts into the depths of rest; fear, indefinable, unaccountable, unknowable, shuddering. Pain begins, for the heart springs into life, and fills the silence with the terror of its beatings, thick, knifing, frightful in its intense longing. Power of mind over soul, power of calm over fear avail nothing; suspense and misery, locked arm in arm, pervade stillness until all things else become subordinate, unnoticed.

Centuries drift away, and the giddy, old reprobate earth, dying a hideous, ghastly death, with but one solitary human to shudder in unison with its last throes, to bask in the last pale rays of a cold sun, to inhale the last breath of metallic atmosphere; totters, reels, falls into space, and is no more. Peal out, ye brazen bells, peal out the requiem of the sinner. Roll your mournful tones into the ears of the saddened angels, weeping with wing-covered eyes. Toll the requiem of the sinner, sinking swiftly, sobbingly into the depths of time's ocean.

Down, down, until the great groans which arose from the domes and Ionic roofs about me told that the sad old earth sought rest in eternity while the universe shrugged its shoulders over the loss of another star.

And now, the great invisible fear became apparent, tangible, for all the sins, the woes, the miseries, the dreads, the dismal achings and throbbings, the dreariness and gloom of the lost star came together and like a huge genie took form and hideous shape which slowly approached me and hovered about my couch in fearful menace.

Oh, shining web of hair, burst loose your bonds and bid me move. Oh, time, cease not your calculations, but speed me on to deliverance. Oh, silence, vast, immense, infuse into your soul some sound other than the heavy throbbing of this fast disintegrating heart. Oh, pitiless stone arches, let fall your crushing weight upon this Stygian monster.

I pray to time, to eternity, to the frozen eons of the past. Useless. I am seized, forced to open my cold lips; there is agony — supreme, mortal agony of nerve tension, and wrenching of vitality. I struggle, scream, and clutching the monster with superhuman strength, fling him aside, and rise, bleeding, screaming, but triumphant, and keenly mortal in every vein, alive and throbbing with consciousness and pain.

No, it was not opium, nor nightmare, but chloroform, a dentist, three obstinate molars, a pair of forceps, and a lively set of nerves.

SALAMMBO BY GUSTAVE FLAUBERT

Like unto the barbaric splendor, the clashing of arms, the flashing of jewels, so is this book, full of brightness that dazzles, yet does not weary, of rich mosaic beauty of sensuous softness. Yet, with it all, there is a singular lack of elevation of thought and expression. Everything tends to degrade, to drag the mind to a worse than earthly level. The crudity of the warriors, the minute description of the battles, the leper, Hann. Even the sensual love scene of Salammbo and Matho, and the rites of Taint and Moloch. Possibly this is due to the peculiar shortness and crispness of the sentences, and the painstaking attention to details. Nothing is left for the imagination to complete. The slightest turn of the hand, the smallest bit of tapestry and armor — all is described until one's brain becomes weary with the scintillating flash of minutia. Such careful attention wearies and disappoints, and sometimes, instead of photographing the scenes indelibly upon the mental vision, there ensues only a confused mass of armor and soldiers, plains and horses.

But the description of action and movement are incomparable, resembling somewhat, in the rush and flow of words, the style of Victor Hugo; the breathless rush and fire, the restrained passion and fury of a master.

Throughout the whole book this peculiarity is noticeable. There are no dissertations, no pauses for the author to express his opinions, no stoppages to reflect. We are rushed onward with almost breathless haste, and many times are fain to pause and re-read a sentence, a paragraph, sometimes a whole page. Like the unceasing motion of a column of artillery in battle, like the roar and fury of the Carthaginian's elephant, so is the torrent of Flaubert's eloquence — majestic, grand, intense, with nobility, sensuous, but never sublime, never elevating, never delicate.

As an historian, Flaubert would have ranked high, at least in impartiality. Not once in the whole volume does he allow his prejudices, his opinions, his sentiments to crop out. We lose complete sight of the author in his work. With marvellous fidelity he explains the movements, the vices and the virtues of each party, and with Shakespearean tact, he conceals his identity, so that we are troubled with none of that Byronic vice of 'dipping one's pen into one's self.'

Still, for all the historian's impartiality, he is just a trifle incorrect, here and there. The ancients mention no aqueduct in or near Carthage. Hann was not crucified outside of Tunis. The incident of the Carthaginian women cutting off their tresses to furnish strings for bows and catapults is generally conceded to have occurred during the latter portion of the third Punic War. And still another difficulty presents itself. Salammbo was supposed to have been the only daughter of Hamilcar. According to Flaubert she dies unmarried, or rather on her wedding day, and yet historians tell us that after the death of the elder Barca, Hannibal was brought up and watched over by Hamilcar's son-in-law, Hasdrubal. Can it be possible that the crafty Numidian King, Nari Havas, is the intrepid, fearless and whole-souled Hasdrubal? Or is it only another deviation from the beaten track of history? In a historical novel, however, and one so evidently arranged for dramatic effects, such lapses from the truth only heighten the interest and kindle the imagination to a brighter flame.

The school of realism of which Zola, Tolstoi, De Maupassant, and others of that ilk are followers, claims its descent from the author of Salammbo. Perhaps their claim is well-founded, perhaps not. We are inclined to believe that it is, for every page in this novel is crowded with details, often disgusting, which are generally left out in ordinary works. The hideous deformity, the rottenness and repulsiveness of the leper Hann is brought out in such vivid detail that we sicken and fain would turn aside in disgust. But go where one will, the ghastly, quivering, wretched picture is always before us in all its filth and splendid misery. The reeking horrors of the battle-fields, the disgusting details of the army imprisoned in the defile of the battle-axe, the grimness of the sacrifices to the blood-thirsty god, Moloch, the wretchedness of Hamilcar's slaves are presented with every ghastly detail, with every degrading trick of expression. Picture after picture of misery and foulness arises and pursues us as the grim witches pursued the hapless Tam O'Shanter, clutching us in ghastly arms, clinging to us with grim and ghoulish tenacity.

Viewing the character through the genteel crystal of nineteenth century civilization, they are all barbarous, unnatural, intensified. But considering the age in which they lived — the tendencies of that age, the gods they worshipped, the practices in which they indulged — they are all true to life, perfect in the depiction of their natures. Spendius is a true Greek, crafty, lying, deceitful, ungrateful. Hamilcar needs no novelist to crystalize his character in words, he always remains the same Hamilcar of history, so it is with Hann. But to Flaubert alone are we indebted for the hideous realism of his external aspect. Matho is a dusky son of Libya — fierce, passionate, resentful, unbridled in his speech and action, swept by the hot breath of furious love. Salammbo, cold and strange delving deep in the mysticism of the Carthaginian gods, living apart from human passions in her intense love for the goddess, Tanit. Salammbo, in the earnest excess of her religious fervor, eagerly accepting the mission given her by the puzzled Saracharabim. Salammbo, twining the gloomy folds of the python about her perfumed limbs. Salammbo, resisting, then yielding to the fierce love of Matho. Salammbo, dying when her erstwhile lover expires. Salammbo, in all her many phases reminds us of some early Christian martyr or saint, though the sweet spirit of the Great Teacher is hidden in the punctual devotion to the mysterious rites of Tanit. She is an inexplicable mixture of the tropical exotic and the frigid snow-flower. A rich and rare growth that attracts and repulses, that interests and absorbs, that we admire without loving, detest without hating.

END